"Do I scare you?" Drake asked.

"A little," Marly murmured. "But it's nothing you did. It's just... There's a lot of stuff I'm working through," she told him. "Sometimes it hits me harder than others."

Drake knew all too well about painful memories creeping up at random times, cutting you off at the knees when you least expected it. But he'd learned to conquer those demons when they threatened him. He was stronger than he'd been a year ago, and he wanted to help Marly build on her strength.

"I'm a pretty good listener," he said.

Drake stepped closer, fully aware that he was teetering on a thin line with her emotions. But that damn pull between them crackled in the air, making him want to hold her, to offer some sort of comfort.

"Sometimes it only looks like there's no hope," he told her. "Trust me."

Damp eyes came up to meet his and the punch to the gut was swift and unexpected.

THE ST. JOHNS OF STONEROCK:
Three rebellious brothers come home to stay.

Dear Reader,

Welcome back to The St. Johns of Stonerock. If you read *Dr. Daddy's Perfect Christmas*, you've already met the hunky firefighting brother, Drake St. John. Drake is such a special hero and holds a special place in my heart. He's suffering from a loss so severe and crippling, yet he's trying to move on. When he meets Marly, the quiet, intriguing nurse, he instantly recognizes another broken soul...and what hero can turn away from a distressed damsel?

Marly isn't too keen on her instant attraction to Drake. With settling into a new town, worrying her past will catch up with her and trying to provide a stable home for her spunky six-year-old, Marly tries to push away her unwanted emotions. Easier said than done, especially when her daughter sees Drake as a real-life hero.

I hope Drake steals your heart the way he captured Marly's. He is determined not to let pain from the past ruin the beautiful love they have found in each other. The St. Johns are a loyal group of brothers and nobody will sever the bond of this dynamic family or stand between them and the women they love.

If you enjoy Drake's story, stay tuned for Cameron's!

Happy reading,

Jules Bennett

The Fireman's Ready-Made Family

Jules Bennett

⬦ **HARLEQUIN**® SPECIAL EDITION®

Recycling programs
for this product may
not exist in your area.

ISBN-13: 978-0-373-65868-8

The Fireman's Ready-Made Family

Copyright © 2015 by Jules Bennett

This edition published by arrangement with Harlequin Books S.A.

For questions and comments about the quality of this book, please contact us at CustomerService@Harlequin.com.

Printed in U.S.A.

Award-winning author **Jules Bennett** is no stranger to romance—she met her husband when she was only fourteen. After dating through high school, the two married. He encouraged her to chase her dream of becoming an author. Jules has now published nearly thirty novels. She and her husband are living their own happily-ever-after while raising two girls. Jules loves to hear from readers through her website, julesbennett.com, her Facebook fan page or on Twitter.

Books by Jules Bennett

Harlequin Special Edition

The St. Johns of Stonerock

Dr. Daddy's Perfect Christmas

Harlequin Desire

The Barrington Trilogy

When Opposites Attract...
Single Man Meets Single Mom
Carrying the Lost Heir's Child

Visit the Author Profile page at Harlequin.com for more titles.

I dedicate this book to all the real-life heroes who shine a light into someone's darkened world. May you ever be blessed.

Chapter One

The firefighter was back.

Once again dressed in his blue cargo pants and matching blue polo with the Stonerock, Tennessee, fire department's seal embroidered on the left side of his chest…a chest that really maxed out the material of his shirt.

But muscles meant something entirely different now. A few years ago the well-sculpted body of a man would have had her appreciating the view. Unfortunately, her world had been vastly changed six months earlier, and now muscles, power and strength only reminded her of the scars she'd be wearing forever.

Pediatric nurse Marly Haskins moved farther into the private room of her six-year-old patient. The young boy had been badly burned in a house fire only a few days ago. The doctors were waiting to see how the wounds healed and pumping him full of antibiotics to ward off infection before discussing the use of skin grafts on his arm and torso.

Marly's heart ached for the boy, who had started kindergarten with her daughter, Willow, just a few weeks ago. This little guy should be at school running around on the playground, not recovering from a fire that had claimed his home.

As Marly approached the side of the bed, the firefighter raised his gaze to her. Those piercing blue eyes shouldn't make her belly do flips, but she couldn't control her body's reaction. Her mind, though… Her mind knew better than to be impressed by beauty, brawn and silent allure.

"Let me know if I'm in your way," he told her as his eyes drifted back down to the sleeping boy. "I just wanted to see him before my shift."

Other than family, no one had been by to see Jeremy. Marly had been told by Jeremy's parents that the fire chief was a close friend of the family and he would be visiting often. Marly didn't know his name, just that he was the chief—another man in a powerful position. A man whose physical appeal had her wishing she wasn't so cynical and jaded. Would she always look at muscles and power as a bad thing?

"I'm just giving him another round of antibiotics," she told him, hoping he didn't want small talk and thankful that he stood on the other side of the bed.

Marly wiped the boy's port with an alcohol pad and

injected the medicine before slipping the needle into the biohazard bin on the wall.

Jeremy slept peacefully, due in part to the pain medication he was on. This was the hard part of her job. The part where she imagined how easily this could be her daughter lying here and how fortunate Marly was that Willow was in school right now, safe and having fun with her friends...just as any five-year-old child should.

"I'm Drake, by the way."

Marly turned her attention back to the imposing man. With wide shoulders stretching his polo, his tall, lean build and those captivating baby blues, the mesmerizing stranger silently demanded attention. Her pulse kicked up whenever they made eye contact, and she hated the thread of fear that niggled at her.

He reminded her too much of her past life—a life she was still trying to escape. A life she was privately rebuilding one day at a time.

Guilt slid through her. Judging a stranger wasn't quite fair. After all, a stranger hadn't hurt her. The man who'd vowed to love, honor and cherish her, though, had nearly destroyed her.

"I'm Marly."

"I know." With a soft smile, he nodded toward her badge clipped on the pocket of her puppy-printed smock top. "I should've introduced myself before now."

"You were preoccupied." The man may be menacing in size, but the worry lines between thick, dark brows spoke of vulnerability. "I understand you and Jeremy's parents are friends."

Nodding, Drake gripped the edge of the bed rail and

stared down at the boy. "Yeah. I graduated with his dad, Shawn. I was on the scene of the fire."

Marly swallowed. Remorse seemed to envelop this man, and there was no doubt he was mentally replaying said scene in his mind.

She'd witnessed that level of sorrow many times over the years as a burn-unit nurse at a children's hospital in Nashville before moving to the suburb of Stonerock. And that was the only reason Jeremy was allowed to stay at this small-town hospital.

"I just wish I could do more," she whispered. "His parents..."

She trailed off, not wanting to get too emotional with this stranger.

Private. That was the theme for this stage in her life. She needed to remain private and locked in her own world, where she could protect herself and her daughter.

"They're having a tough time," he added as he pushed off the rail and came around the edge of the bed. "But you're doing all you can. Keeping their son as comfortable as possible is a blessing to them right now."

Marly nodded, Drake's large, looming presence causing her to step back. He'd done nothing to her, yet she couldn't help that proverbial knee-jerk reaction.

"Are you okay?" he asked, dark brows drawn together.

Easing her side bangs over a tad to keep her scar covered, Marly nodded. "Yeah, just worried. It's hard not to get swept into the lives of my patients."

"That's what makes a good nurse." His soft smile didn't quite reach his eyes, as if the gesture was only for her. "Getting emotionally involved is an occupational hazard."

On one level she knew he understood. After all, they were both public servants and protectors. But on another level, she really didn't want to bond with this man who had her emotions all jumbled up because of his gentleness and potent sex appeal. A lethal combo.

If she wasn't careful, she would find herself slipping into his personal space, and she'd promised herself no more letting herself trust—not yet and probably not for a long, long time. There was too much at stake in her life for her to let her guard down...with anyone.

"When will he be transferred to another hospital with a burn unit?" he asked, crossing his arms over his wide, taut chest.

"We'll have to wait and see if the doctor and his parents decide on the skin grafts."

She tried to ignore the way Drake's size dominated the room. Tried to ignore the way her heart kicked up at the way he seemed to study her.

"I think he needs to be transferred to a hospital that specializes in this type of care," Drake told her, crossing his arms over his wide chest.

Marly wasn't really in the mood to defend her medical position or to discuss her patient's needs with a non-family member. And she definitely wasn't up for being bullied by this man, who no doubt was used to getting his way. She didn't think he was posing for an argument, but he was making it clear his opinion mattered.

"For now he's fine to stay here." She forced herself to meet his gaze. She was no longer that meek woman who was afraid to stand up for herself. "I'm able to care for him because I was a nurse on a burn unit at a larger hospital before I moved here. But if his parents choose for him to have skin grafts, he'll go to a specialist."

"Why the wait?" Drake demanded. "Wouldn't he heal faster if he were with a specialist now?"

Fisting her hands at her sides, Marly shook her head. "The doctors here have Jeremy's best interest in mind, and he's getting the best possible care. And we can't transport him yet anyway."

Drake swore under his breath. "Shawn and Amy are self-employed, and this is really going to hurt them financially on top of all the emotional turmoil they're already experiencing. Never mind the fact they lost their house and they're staying with Shawn's parents."

Okay, so the overpowering man had a soft spot. Seriously, though, how dare he question not only her, but the doctors and Jeremy's parents? Perhaps he was just speaking out of worry, but still, Marly wasn't interested in this chief's medical opinions.

But he was right about one thing. Medical bills were going to flood their lives before they ever got their son home. Marly couldn't imagine the financial strain this would put on the poor family.

Since she'd run from her ex and left behind all the money and flashy things, she was having a hard time adjusting to her single salary, but it was hard to feel sorry for herself when a tragic case like this smacked her in the face with a dose of reality. There was always someone worse off. She had to remind herself of that when pity started to settle in.

"Can I talk to you outside?" Drake asked, intruding on her thoughts.

Surprised at his request, Marly nodded. This was the first real interaction they'd had since Jeremy had been admitted to her unit two days ago. Even though he'd been here both days, she'd made sure to just stick to the pleasantries, getting in and out of Jeremy's room quickly when Drake visited.

They stepped outside the room, and Marly eased the large wooden door closed behind her. Trying to come off as a professional was hard when your hands were shaking, so she crossed her arms over her chest and tipped her head to level his stare.

"Something wrong?" she asked.

"I'm going to be at the station for the next thirty-six hours," he told her, stepping closer so there was only a small gap separating them. "I know Shawn and Amy won't let me know if they need anything, but could you keep an eye on them when they're here? If they need food or a break, could you let me know? I can give you my cell. If I'm not busy I can run over or I can have one of my brothers stop by. I don't want Shawn and Amy to feel like they're in this alone."

Wow. He was serious. The fire chief was ready to drop everything to help a friend in need.

The cynical side of Marly wanted to know if he was using this opportunity for publicity in his position, to look good in the eyes of his superiors. Or did this man actually have that kind of a heart?

She shook off the pull to want to know more. The old Marly would've reached out, but that woman was dead, cut off from all the emotional tugs toward the wounded hearts of others. She had her own heart to heal.

Pulling herself back to his request and his intense stare as he waited on an answer, she smiled. "Of course I can let you know."

His mesmerizing blue eyes continued to study her, and she resisted the urge to reach up and make sure her side bangs were covering her scar. She didn't want to know what he was thinking, didn't want to know what he saw when he looked at her.

Her ex had used her as a trophy, only wanting her to look good at his side and remain silent. But, gone was that quiet, reserved, perfectly-coiffed woman. Now Marly kept her long blond hair in a ponytail, downplayed her voluptuous chest and wore little to no makeup. This was the real Marly Haskins.

"Did you need anything else?" she asked, ready to get out from under his questioning gaze.

Drake shrugged one shoulder. "Just wondering why you look so sad."

Taken aback by his abrupt, imposing question, Marly shook her head. "I'm not sad. I mean, I'm sad for Jeremy and his family, but that's all."

Reaching out, Drake slid a thumb beneath her eye. "No, you've got shadows and there's sadness there."

Swatting his hand away, Marly stepped back. "You don't know me, so I'd appreciate if you didn't analyze me."

Drake raked a hand over his closely cropped dark hair. "My apologies. It's second nature to worry. I just wondered if you were okay."

Was she okay? Far from it. Was she going to spill her heart to this charming stranger? Absolutely not.

But, oh, how she wished she had someone she could open up to. It was so hard being a single mother in the best of times, let alone when trying to keep her abusive ex from discovering where she was living and trying to remain strong and put up a cheerful front for strangers who had no clue the hell she'd endured.

She couldn't focus on Drake or his charms. She needed to concentrate on getting her life back in order and setting a stable foundation for her and her daughter. No room for a handsome stranger with vibrant blue eyes and a killer body. Those two qualities meant nothing in the long run.

Drake reached back and pulled out his wallet, producing a business card. "My cell is on there."

As she slipped the card from his grasp, her fingertips slid across his—the briefest of touches, but enough to have her pulling back. She hadn't touched a man in any way since leaving her husband. Her patients were all children and she'd made a point to stay clear of men at least until her mental state returned to normal.

Scars weren't always just on the outside.

"You sure you're okay?" he asked, brows drawn in as he leaned closer.

Great, now he was seriously concerned about her.

Forcing what she hoped was a convincing smile, Marly nodded. "Fine. Just thinking about Jeremy."

That answer seemed to pacify the chief as he pulled his keys from his other pocket. "Call me anytime. If I can't talk, I won't answer, but leave a message."

Marly nodded, still eager for him to be on his way.

"I'll be back tomorrow," he said.

Yeah, that was what she was afraid of. Each time she saw him her heart would speed up and she'd find herself drawn deeper and deeper into his appeal. That type of mentality was exactly what had gotten her in trouble to begin with.

As Drake walked out of the cheerily painted pediatric unit, Marly couldn't help but watch him go. Those broad shoulders, that uniform, those dark forearms… Drake St. John was all man and all powerful.

But whatever fluttery feeling she got from being around him would just have to be ignored, because no way would she ever get involved with another man—especially one so sexy and powerful. That combination nearly killed her once before.

Chapter Two

Confident that the pretty nurse would notify him if Shawn or Amy needed anything, Drake felt a sliver of satisfaction. Marly, with her wide, chocolate doe eyes, may be leery of him, but he had to assume she'd keep her promise.

He mentally cursed himself for reaching out to her. Good Lord, she'd think he was some type of creep. But he'd seen fear spread through those beautiful eyes of hers when he neared, felt her stiffen beneath his touch.

Drake figured he intimidated her, which was a shame, but he couldn't figure out why. Someone or something had hurt her. The protector in him wanted to keep her safe, as strange as that may sound, considering he barely knew her.

He also couldn't figure out why he kept finding himself thinking about her when he'd leave the hospital. He'd seen her a total of three times—she was fairly new in town, according to all the chatter—but other than that, she was a total stranger he knew nothing about.

Well, he'd known when he'd stepped closer to her earlier that she'd smelled like strawberries; he knew she had a gentle, patient bedside manner; and he knew she was one of the most beautiful women he'd ever seen. With her long blond hair, dark eyes and creamy skin, Marly was a stunner, and he'd never even seen an ounce of makeup on her.

He'd not felt a pull toward another woman in over a year. Not since the day his fiancée had died. He never thought he'd feel for anybody again. In his defense, he'd even been on a couple dates since then, but nothing had ever come of them.

There was something pulling him toward Marly. Whether it was her underlying vulnerability or just the woman in general, he truly had no idea. But he knew he couldn't ignore it, either.

Drake pulled from the hospital parking lot, but before he went to the station, he swung by the courthouse to check on the status of the budget. Granted, the official meeting was tomorrow, but Drake knew the good ol' mayor already had some sort of clue as to what was going on.

Drake mounted the steps, waving to a few city workers as they exited the old historic building. Quickly making his way to the third floor, Drake went in and greeted the elderly secretary, who had been the smiling face of this office for the past forty years. No matter the mayor, Betty May Allen was the right-hand woman. That woman probably held more secrets than the Pentagon.

"Chief St. John." She beamed, sliding down her reading glasses to dangle off the pearl chain. "What can I do for you?"

"Is he in?" Drake asked, nodding toward the closed door.

With the frosted glass and large block lettering, Drake couldn't see.

"He is. You don't have an appointment, do you?" she asked.

"No. I'll just be a minute if he's free."

Betty May slid from behind her L-shaped desk and walked to the door, easing it open a crack. Her silver hair bounced as she nodded and spoke, but he couldn't make out what she was saying.

Turning with her signature smile, Betty May gestured as she opened the door wider. "Go on in, Chief."

"Thank you, ma'am."

Drake closed the door behind him as he took in the overweight, half bald, half comb-over man behind the large mahogany desk. The man looked every bit the part of a small-town mayor. Too bad he didn't play the part like one.

"What can I do for one of my city's finest workers?" Mayor Tipton asked, easing back in his chair hard enough to cause very questionable creaks.

Was it too much to hope the jerk would tip the chair too far and fall backward?

Gripping the back of the leather chair across from

the desk, Drake leveled the man's gaze, refusing to return the smarmy smile. "How's the budget looking? Are we going to be able to bring my men back on board?"

Tipton blinked. "The budget meeting is tomorrow."

Drake never did like a man who couldn't just answer a question straight-out. And he'd certainly never liked this lazy, selfish mayor. He hadn't voted for the man, and he sure as hell hated working under him.

"I'm sure you have some idea," Drake said, clenching the chair and trying to rein in his patience, as he had for several months now. "My department is suffering, and because of that we were shorthanded on the fire at the Adkins' residence on Sunday."

"Yes, I heard all about that." Mayor Tipton leaned forward, propping his flabby forearms on his cluttered desk. "I was told the young boy was severely injured."

Drake swallowed the bitter truth as images of that boy lying beside his bed as flames licked all around his room consumed him. Drake had dragged the unconscious boy out, praying the entire time that he hadn't been too late.

"The city simply doesn't have the extra money," the mayor was saying. "We had to cut somewhere, and unfortunately your department was one of the areas."

Fury bubbled within him, and Drake knew if he didn't leave he'd say something that may get him suspended. But he also wasn't going to back down, not when he had dependable men who needed the income, not to mention men that worked harder in one shift than this mayor did in an entire year.

"Did you happen to look at cutting your own income?

Or maybe the new landscaping in the park? How about those new streetlights that just went up around Main Street? None of that was ever considered? That little boy's injuries lie directly on your head, not mine. I did my job… Can you say the same?"

Drake didn't stop when the mayor pushed his pudgy frame away from the desk and stood. In fact, the idea of the mayor gearing up for the argument was rather amusing and fueled Drake even more. He was definitely teetering on a thin line here.

"Oh, I see where you're coming from," Drake said in his most condescending tone. Sarcasm had always been a strong suit for him and his brothers. "Why pay honest, hardworking men when we can make things pretty? I see that logic. Best to put lives in danger so we can have purple pansies and lantern-style streetlights."

"You better watch yourself, Chief." The mayor's face was slowly turning red, his gobbler neck wiggling back and forth when he spoke. "You always were a smart-mouthed hellion."

Ah, yes. The infamous St. John reputation he and his brothers had had to overcome in order to rise to their rankings in this small town.

Drake didn't care if his character came into play here. He knew he was right and the mayor was flat-out wrong. Drake also didn't care if Tipton got angry. Angry didn't even cover what Drake felt when he thought of the moment he'd had to tell three of his men that they were no longer needed.

"A young boy is lying in the hospital with second- and third-degree burns to his arm and torso," Drake went on, the image alone adding fuel to his anger. "We would've been able to get to him faster had all regular responders been available. We're shorthanded, Mayor, and it's time you realized just how dangerous those cuts have become. The guys left on staff are working overtime, and it's not safe for them or the public to have them so exhausted."

"I sympathize for the boy. The accident was tragic, but I am not to blame here. I have a job, just like you. I suggest you focus on that."

A whole new level of rage slid through him. "Are you suggesting I didn't do my job?"

With a slight shrug, the mayor merely stared across the desk.

Yeah, if he didn't leave, Drake would get fired...at the very least, because the urge to punch the guy in the face was too strong. Fortunately Drake had self-control and actually cared about protecting the people in this town. That right there proved he'd overcome his rebellious days. Once upon a time Drake and his brothers would punch first and discuss later.

"One way or another, my men will come back to work," Drake assured him. "Your term is almost up. Then we'll see who really cares about the safety of the citizens."

"Are you threatening me?"

With a slow grin, Drake raised his hands, palms out. "Just stating a fact. The voters will take care of you."

And with that he walked out, nodding to Betty May, who was wide-eyed, no doubt hearing the heated encounter—not Drake's first with the mayor, but perhaps the most hate filled.

Drake marched all the way back to his truck and slammed the door. Damn it. He had to figure out a way to get the city to allow him to hire his men back on. The men who were currently working were maxed out. They were tired and all feeling the extra stress… not good when lives were on the line every single day.

Drake clenched the steering wheel and stared out the windshield toward the old fountain in the distance at the park.

Andrea had loved that fountain. Had always said if she got married she'd do it there in the summer with all the beauty of the tall old oaks surrounding her.

Drake had every intention of giving her that dream. He'd had every intention of giving her everything she'd ever wanted.

But that dream had died in a fiery crash.

Starting the engine, Drake forced out the crippling images of that day. His counselor was right. Focusing on the past wouldn't help him rebuild for a better future. And he knew that Andrea would want him to move on; she'd want him to live his life. Besides, he had a department he needed to fight for and a boy in the hospital he cared about.

Which brought him right back to the pretty nurse who seemed a bit skittish when he was around. Her beauty was rather shocking, and Drake hadn't felt a physical pull toward anyone since Andrea. Which only made his mixed-up emotions even more confusing.

How could he find another woman so appealing in

such a short time? Should he ask her out? He had to keep trying his hand at dating if he wanted to truly move on.

But Marly was afraid of something. Perhaps he should approach this on a friendship level, because Drake knew one thing. He had to find out what had put the shadows beneath her pretty eyes.

Marly was thankful her supervisor gave her a few hours off to chaperone Willow on the kindergarten field trip. Marly knew it was going to be tough to hold a full-time job and be the parent Willow needed, especially after removing Willow from the only home she'd known.

So far Willow was adjusting perfectly, and today's field trip to the fire department was all her sweet little five-year-old could talk about this morning.

Marly left work early and pulled into the department lot just after the bus did. It didn't take long for Marly to zero in on the chief, and she cursed herself for instantly seeking him out.

Drake stepped up to the open doors of the bus and greeted the kids with a wide grin as they bounced off the last step and raced across the lot to the closest shiny red truck. Another group of men in blue polos and matching pants herded the children to the grassy area, where they had them take a seat.

As Marly got out of her SUV, her eyes locked on the chief. She hadn't seen him since that awkward moment in the hallway two days ago. He hadn't popped in yesterday like he'd said he would, and she hated that she'd had a sliver of disappointment when her shift had ended and she hadn't seen him.

Marly crossed the parking lot and headed toward the front of the bus to wait for Willow. Before she could spot her daughter, Drake raised his head. Even with his dark aviator sunglasses on, she knew he was looking right at her.

Sweltering heat from the late-summer sun did nothing to prevent the chills from racing through her. The instant reaction her body took to this man was unexplainable and unwanted. Yes, at one time she would've loved to have felt chills over the thought of a man like Drake looking at her, but that was years ago, before she'd married a monster.

Trusting her judgment now wasn't the smartest move. She needed to regroup, build a solid life on her own before trying to appreciate a man like Drake. Her personal life would have to come later—much later.

Such a shame, though. She didn't remember the last time a man had looked at her and made her feel anything but fear.

"Mama!"

Marly smiled as Willow came running up to her. "Come on." Willow started tugging on Marly's hand. "They're going to let us squirt the hoses in a minute, and the teacher said we may get to climb inside a truck."

Laughing, Marly allowed herself to be pulled toward the other smiling, wiggly kids. She passed by Drake, earning a devastating smile and a nod of his head.

"Marly."

Unable to help herself, Marly returned his smile. "Chief St. John."

Mercy. Just passing by the man and his spicy scent had Marly wondering where on earth her head had gone. Hadn't she scolded herself already? Physical attraction wasn't something she could indulge in. But just because she didn't plan on doing anything about this sudden on-slaught of emotions didn't mean she couldn't appreciate the view of such a spectacular man.

"I want to sit in the front," Willow said, taking a seat beside a little boy wearing his school spirit T-shirt. "This is my friend Alan. Just stand over there with the other moms, but watch me when I squirt the hose. Okay?"

"All right, sweetie," Marly agreed.

She stepped aside, but not too close to the other moms. She was only here to see her daughter, help if needed and snap some pictures of her baby's first field trip. What she wasn't here to do was make friends with other moms or spend her time fantasizing about Chief Drake St. John.

But as she watched him interact with the children, she found herself softening toward this local hero even more. The children all stared up at him with wide eyes as he projected his strong voice over the young crowd. They were his captive audience as he discussed how firefighters rescued people when they were scared and needed help.

Within moments he had donned full firefighting gear to show them how they may look scary, but all the equipment was to keep them safe so they could help others in danger.

That instant, Marly found herself drawn deeper into his world. Whether she wanted to or not, she was mesmerized and hung on his every word…just like the children.

Great. Now what? The emotions were there. No matter how she'd tried to dodge and deny them, they were in the forefront of her mind. So what on earth did she do with that revelation?

Drake absolutely loved this part of his job. He loved the interaction with the kids, enjoyed seeing their smiling faces as he explained the different tools on the different fire trucks; he even loved letting them play with the fire hose.

But today, all of that faded in the background. Marly had a child—a little girl who looked exactly like her. Once his initial shock wore off, he realized he was staring like a fool.

Drake wasn't sure if he was more shocked at the fact she had a child or the fact she was smiling so widely, so beautifully. He'd not seen her so happy before. Of course, he'd only seen her in her element at work, caring for Jeremy.

The second he'd spotted her, his heart had tightened, but when her face had lit up at the sight of her little girl, Drake had literally felt that punch to the gut he'd heard his brother Eli talk about.

Now that the children had gone through their tour and were starting to line back up for the bus, Drake realized Marly had pretty much stayed in the shadows. He'd caught her snapping photos of her daughter, and now she was holding the little girl, kissing her on the cheek. Drake lurched forward. He couldn't let an opportunity pass him by.

"Would you like a picture together?" he offered.

Marly's head whipped around. "Drake."

"You know the chief?" Willow asked, wide-eyed and obviously impressed. "Why didn't you say so? That's the coolest!"

Drake laughed. "Maybe your mom could bring you back sometime. I'm sure I can find time to take you for a ride in the fire engine."

The little girl's mouth dropped. "If you're kidding, Chief, I'm gonna be sad."

Drake couldn't help but reach out and give a tug on one of her long blond ponytails. "I would never kid someone so eager to learn about firefighting. But you have to promise one thing."

"Anything," she squealed and wiggled in Marly's arms. "What is it?"

"You won't try to take my job once you learn all this stuff."

He forced his eyes to stay locked onto the little girl, which wasn't a hardship because she was so adorable. But he could feel Marly's gaze on him, and he wanted to turn and see those dark eyes of hers.

"I promise, Chief," the little girl assured.

"Call me Drake." He held out a hand for her to shake. "And your first name is?"

Her tiny hand slid into his and she squeezed. "Willow."

"Nice to meet you, Willow. Your bus is loading, so how about I take a picture of you and your mom in front of the station so you guys can always remember this day?"

"Oh, Drake, you don't have to," Marly protested.

He cut his gaze to hers; thankfully he'd removed his sunglasses so he could see her with no barrier. "I know I don't have to. I want to."

Marly smiled as she handed over her phone. "In that case, we'd love a picture."

Drake made sure he took a couple. He knew from experience that most women wanted options. Sweet Willow, with her golden pigtails, gave her mommy a big hug and scrambled down to race to the bus.

Marly waved goodbye and turned to Drake. "Thank you. You're really good with children."

Shrugging, Drake rested his hands on his hips. "Kids are great. You just have to know how to treat them."

A shadow passed over Marly's eyes. "Do you have kids?" she asked, raising her arm to shield the sun from her eyes.

He thought of Andrea, of the dreams they'd had. The family they'd planned.

"No," he told her. "I'm an uncle to a beautiful baby girl, but none of my own yet."

Sliding her phone back into her smock pocket, Marly started to pass him. "Well, I need to get back to work. Thanks again for being so great with all the kids, and especially Willow."

"I meant what I said." He turned to meet her stare as she started to walk away. "Anytime you see my black truck here, swing in, and if we're not busy I'd love to give her a ride on the engine. I know she'd enjoy it."

Marly studied him for a moment before a corner of her mouth kicked up. "You really do love kids, don't you?"

Taken back by her odd question, Drake nodded. "What's not to love?"

There it was again, that ghost of an emotion taking over, and Marly's smile turned sad in an instant. "I agree. See you around, Chief."

Drake watched until Marly was in her car and headed down the street. A hand slapped him hard on the shoulder, and Drake turned to see one of his men grinning.

"She's a looker, Chief."

Drake nodded. No sense in denying the truth.

"Gonna ask her out?"

Shaking his head, Drake laughed. "I have no clue what I'm going to do. No clue."

And that was the honest truth. Because on one hand he wanted to see Marly on a personal level, but on the other hand she was scared of something—or maybe someone.

The pull Drake felt toward her, though, was only getting stronger. As much as he wanted to see more of the beautiful pediatric nurse, he also knew he needed to take things slow.

After all, he was still on shaky ground himself in regards to relationships.

Chapter Three

Those piercing blue eyes had penetrated her once again. If Marly thought Drake a big man before, now that she'd seen him in full gear, he was even more impressive. She knew broad shoulders lay beneath that bulky coat, and his towering height was only emphasized by his helmet.

What drew her to powerful men? Although she had to admit, Kevin's power was used to blackmail and lie to get what he wanted. From the little she'd seen of Drake, the man genuinely cared for his job, the people he encountered. Drake certainly didn't seem the type to use others for a publicity stunt.

Marly steered her car back into the hospital lot and found an open spot. Now that Willow had been given the invitation to go to the fire station, no doubt the rambunctious little girl would ask every two minutes when they were going.

Which meant Marly would have to go back and witness Drake in all his gorgeous glory. A part of her so wanted to address the tension that settled between them each time they were within breathing space of each other, but at the same time, she wanted to deny any attraction existed. She wanted to ignore the desire that seemed to creep up on her when she didn't have the mental strength to stop it.

Killing her engine, Marly sighed and rested her head against the steering wheel. No matter her sudden attraction to Drake, she had a war she was still fighting, and that had to come before anything else.

When her phone chimed to signal a text, Marly pulled the cell from her purse and cringed at the screen.

Call me. You can't avoid me forever.

That didn't mean she wouldn't try like hell.

Tossing her phone back in her purse, Marly stepped out of her car, welcoming the warmth of the midday sun. When she'd left Nashville, she'd found enough courage to force Kevin into letting her go, taking Willow and not disclosing her whereabouts in exchange for the pictures she had promised would not go to the newspaper or other media outlets.

Kevin didn't know she'd gone to the police... Of course, she figured he knew now. No doubt some corrupt cop who was friends of the family had called Kevin moments after Marly had left. Marly knew the power

Kevin's family held, so she also knew that was probably why the Nashville Police Department hadn't returned her calls and she'd heard no more on her case... if there even was a case.

Marly figured the only reason Kevin hadn't hired a PI and traced her phone was because of his powerful status and the fact that he tended to avoid public conflict. For once, his social standing was working in her favor.

Even with the sun beating down on her, she trembled. There was no way in hell she'd ever return to Kevin. If she had to stay on the run the rest of her life to protect her child, then so be it. She would never be another man's punching bag or pawn again.

The day after the field trip, Marly was stepping out of Jeremy's room when Drake came striding through the bright yellow walls of the pediatric unit. The cheery surroundings made him seem less intimidating, but the man's impressive size still dominated the space.

When his gaze met hers, his lips spread wide in a smile that hit her hard. Then she spotted the small stuffed Dalmatian in his hand and she couldn't help but return the grin. Why was she softening toward this man so fast? She'd learned her lesson, right? Just because a man was charming and good-looking didn't mean he treated women right when no one was looking.

But there was still that nugget of doubt that kept telling her Drake was nothing like the man she'd married. Nothing.

"You carry toys everywhere you go?" she asked, once he closed the gap between them.

Glancing down at the toy in question, Drake shrugged. When his eyes met hers once again, they held as his voice lowered. "My toys are a bit larger than this."

She shivered at the veiled flirting and innuendo. The part deep inside her that had thought no man would ever find her attractive again sparked to life. For so long she'd not even been given a second thought, other than being used as a pawn or publicity stunt.

But Drake had a way of making her feel... Just feel, and that was something she'd have to get used to if she was going to keep seeing him in this small town.

"I assume that's for our patient?"

With a nod, Drake asked, "How's he doing today?"

"Good. Amy just stepped out to get a bite to eat and Shawn ran home to shower. I nearly had to bribe them to take care of themselves."

Drake swallowed hard, glancing away.

"You okay?" she asked.

"Yeah, I just... This whole situation kills me. I don't know what to say to Shawn. Words won't fix what happened." He shook his head. "Talking to people after accidents is part of my job, yet this is on a whole new level of difficulty. Shawn and I are friends."

"You saved their son's life," Marly pointed out. "They're grateful."

"I know they are," he told her, waiting until another nurse went by before he continued, "I'm thankful I got to him in time, but the entire situation just sucks."

"You didn't tell me you were the one who pulled Jeremy from the fire. Amy was telling me earlier how she doesn't know what they would've done without you."

Drake's eyes held hers, but he didn't utter a word. A true hero was someone who didn't boast or brag of his achievements. A true hero did his job, though fear may overpower him. A true hero cared for others, put their needs first, even at the risk of being injured himself.

And before her stood a true hero.

"You can go in and see him, but I'll need to put the toy at the nurse's station with his other things. We've been keeping all of the balloons and flowers out here since his room is set up for his special needs due to the burns."

He passed the stuffed dog over, and Marly was careful not to let her hands brush his again. The less contact with this potent man the better. He was already wreaking havoc on her nerves and consuming way too much of her mind and she barely knew him.

"Go on in," Marly said, afraid of just how fast she was becoming infatuated with the town fire chief. "I'll be back in a bit."

She quickly rushed off and went straight to the employees' restroom. Flicking the lock, Marly sank against the back of the door. Drake St. John was becoming a bigger issue than she'd first thought.

When he'd first come into the pediatric unit she realized he was probably there to check on the boy because that fell in line with being the chief. But then when he'd been there nearly every day, he was great with Willow and now he'd brought a stuffed animal for Jeremy... He was becoming more and more real.

Marly sighed. Real? That sounded ridiculous. Of course he was real, but now he was even more genuine and melting away that layer she'd formed around her heart. She needed to be on guard, not to start feeling all schoolgirl over a handsome, charming fire chief.

No doubt, his physical appeal couldn't be denied, but how could she allow herself to be so taken with him so fast? She'd learned her lesson—the hard way—on big, powerful men. Right now she had to focus on rebuilding her new life and trying to keep custody of Willow. Kevin wouldn't stop at sending texts and voice mails. He'd take action by hiring a PI, if he hadn't already.

But it was getting harder and harder to focus when Drake came around. Between his easy rapport with Willow and his dedication to Jeremy's welfare, there was so much more to Drake than power.

Perhaps that was what scared her most.

Marly looked at herself in the mirror. In twenty-six years, she'd been through too much. All she wanted was happiness, a settled life in which she felt safe, protected and secure. Not only for herself, but also for her daughter.

She eased her blond hair back, facing the ugly, jagged scar that ran down her temple. Vanity had never been her thing, so the physical image wasn't what bothered her. Kevin's fists had taken so much more than physical beauty. They had taken away her freedom, her sense of self-worth and her courage. But she was getting those back. No way would she give Kevin the satisfaction of stealing everything from her.

Including her daughter.

Her eyes roamed down to the small scar on her chin. That one was impossible to hide, but at least it was on the underside, so it wasn't as noticeable and easier to chalk up to a fall from childhood.

Adjusting her hair back in place, she took a deep, calming breath and headed back to work. At some point she'd have to face the fact that she was finding herself more and more intrigued by—and dare she say attracted to—Drake.

She couldn't act on her unstable emotions. After all, how could she trust anything she felt after her poor judgment regarding her ex? On the other hand, she couldn't keep lying to herself about this invisible tug whenever Drake was around. She was a woman who had desires and eyes, for pity's sake. How could any woman not do a double take at Drake? And after that double take, the real problems started. Because the looks didn't make the man…the big heart and devastating smile did.

Drake eyed the young boy lying in the sterile bed wearing a sheet up to his waist, dressings wrapped around his torso and his left arm. Drake's heart literally ached for Jeremy, Shawn and Amy. Such a beautiful family living in a small town like so many others around the country, and now fate had turned their world upside down.

Someone needed to step up and help them. There was no way Shawn and Amy could take on this financial burden alone. Wasn't that what people in small towns did? Rallied behind each other when one of them was hurting? Besides, they needed mental support, as well. No one should ever go through a trauma like this alone.

Drake figured he'd get the ball rolling in the direction of a fund-raiser to assist Shawn and Amy. He couldn't just sit back and do nothing.

Drake wanted to drag the mayor from behind his desk and his cushy leather chair and show him the ramifications of cutting good, hardworking firefighters. Drake had zero tolerance for that man, and this was just another reason Drake couldn't wait until the next election when hopefully a new mayor was sworn in…a mayor who actually cared about the people of the town.

When Drake stepped from the room and eased the door shut behind him, Marly was nowhere to be seen. He walked up to the nurses' station and was greeted by a middle-aged lady wearing character scrubs with her hair in a tight, high bun.

Balloons, teddy bears and flowers were piled high on the back counter. Drake figured all of those gifts were for Jeremy, since Drake saw the stuffed toy he brought nestled in the mix.

"Excuse me," he said, leaning an arm on the top of the high counter. "Is Marly busy?"

"I haven't seen her for a couple of minutes. Maybe she's in the break room." The lady turned, gesturing behind the desk to a narrow hall. "It's the first door on the right. Go on in."

Drake smiled. "Thank you, ma'am."

Drake figured wearing his department logo on his shirt had gotten him the pass to the employee area. He went around the desk and into the break room but didn't see Marly. As he turned to leave, Marly rounded the corner to enter the room and plowed right into him.

Instincts had him reaching out, gripping her arms tight in an attempt to steady her. The second he grabbed her, she screamed and jumped back.

The color had gone from her face, and Drake held his hands out to his side. "Are you okay?"

A shaky hand came up to her heart as she nodded, her eyes not quite meeting his.

"Marly." He eased closer. The disturbing look in her eyes wasn't just shock at finding him in here, this was pure fear. "Come in and sit down."

After a moment of silence, she sought his eyes and shook her head. "No, no. I'm okay."

"You've gone pale and you're shaking." He started to reach for her, but she moved back. Dread settled deep in his stomach. "Are you afraid of me?"

Marly closed her eyes and sighed. "No," she whispered.

Drake had no clue what demons she was battling before his eyes, so he remained silent. God knew he'd never wanted anyone to witness his rough moments after Andrea's accident.

It wasn't long before she raked a hand down her face and opened her eyes. With her shoulders back and head high, Drake knew she'd pushed through whatever hell she'd entered into moments ago.

"Sorry," she told him, trying hard for a smile, but failing. "You just caught me off guard."

And she didn't like to be touched, apparently. There was a story there...a story he feared would make him want to protect her at all costs and dig even deeper into her world.

"It's okay," he assured her. "I was just heading out, but I wanted to run something by you."

Nodding, she gestured toward the table and chairs. "Let's have a seat."

He moved out of her way, letting her go where she wanted before he pulled out a chair across from her. The last thing he needed was her to worry about being alone with him. He wanted to gain her trust, and after what he'd just witnessed, he feared getting into Marly's inner circle would take more time and patience than he'd first thought...but something told him she would be worth the effort.

"Is something wrong?" she asked, lacing her fingers on the tabletop.

"No, I just wanted to discuss Jeremy with you."

He hadn't realized he was going to bring up the fund-raiser with Marly, but he found that he wanted to include her in the planning.

"You and I are both worried about his parents financially, especially since the doctor decided he'll have to have grafts. When he's transported to the specialist, Shawn and Amy will have added travel expenses." He eased forward in his seat, resting his forearms on the table. "What if we did a fund-raiser for them?"

Marly's eyes widened. "We? Like you and me?"

Smiling, Drake nodded. "Well, yeah. I'd appreciate your opinion. But if you don't have the time, I understand."

Marly rested her chin on her palm and seemed to process the idea. Drake didn't know what had come over him, why he wanted to work with her on this project, but he found himself holding his breath until she nodded with a smile.

"I'll do it. Willow can help, too. We could all work on this." A slow smile lit up her face. "What did you have in mind?"

Yeah, he hadn't got that far yet, but now that she was all in, he had to come up with something.

"I'm not sure yet," he told her honestly. "Why don't I come over and we can discuss it more? I'm off until tomorrow."

When she remained silent, he knew she was battling that same demon as moments ago. Someone had hurt her, someone had scared her, and he damn well wanted to know who. Another invisible tug pulled him toward her whether he liked it or not…whether he was ready or not.

He didn't want to push her, didn't want to scare her, but at the same time, he needed to let her know he wasn't going anywhere and he wasn't treating her with kid gloves. She was the type of woman who needed to find her courage again, and he'd damn well be the man to help her.

"I can bring pizza so you don't have to worry about dinner," he told her. "Willow seems like a kid who would love pizza."

"As if she didn't think you were cool enough already after the invitation back to the station," she told him with a slight grin. "I get off work at four and I need to pick her up from the sitter, so why don't you come over about four-thirty?"

Feeling as if he'd truly accomplished something, Drake came to his feet. "Sounds good. Any special requests for toppings?"

Marly rose as well and shook her head. "I'll eat anything, and if Willow doesn't like it, she'll just pick it off. But, if you want to gain extra points, she really loves banana peppers."

"I'm all about scoring extra points."

When Drake stepped closer, Marly's eyes widened as her head tilted up so she could look him in the face. That underlying vulnerability kept eating at him. He had no clue what she'd been through, it was none of his business, but he had a feeling whatever war she was battling, she wasn't finished yet.

Everything in him wanted to get to know her more. He knew he needed to move on, knew Andrea would want him to find happiness. And Marly was the first woman since Andrea who had sparked this much emotion inside him, so he couldn't ignore it.

What if he wasn't ready? What if he tried to get closer to a woman and he couldn't follow through?

Damn it, he couldn't live in fear. He wouldn't live in fear. Going slow with Marly, working on gaining her trust, was the best step to take.

He focused on those dark eyes as they looked back up at him. "Can I ask you something?"

Her gaze held his as she nodded.

"Do I scare you?"

"A little," she murmured. "It's nothing you did. It's just…"

Unable to help himself, he rested his hand on her shoulder, keeping his touch light when she started to tense. "I don't want you uncomfortable around me, Marly."

"There's a lot of stuff I'm working through," she told him. "Sometimes it hits me harder than others."

Drake knew all too well about painful memories creeping up at random times, cutting you off at the knees when you least expected it. He'd be lying if he said he was over Andrea's death, but he'd at least learned to conquer those demons when they threatened him. He was stronger than a year ago, and he wanted to help Marly build on her strength.

"I'm a pretty good listener," he said, giving her shoulder a slight squeeze, pleased when she didn't pull away.

"I'm sure you are, but I…" She shook her head and sighed.

Drake stepped closer, fully aware that he was teetering on a thin line where her emotions were concerned. But that damn pull between them crackled in the air, making him want to hold her, to offer some comfort.

His other hand came up to cup her other shoulder as he eased forward. "Sometimes it only looks as though there's no hope," he told her. "Trust me."

Damp eyes came up to meet his, and the punch to the gut was swift and unexpected.

"My trust was shattered," she whispered, keeping her wet eyes locked on his. "I can't face this… I can't get close to anyone, if that's what you were thinking."

Shocked that she'd called him out, Drake slid his hands from her shoulders and let them drop.

"I wasn't looking for anything more than friendship, Marly. I want to help Jeremy and I'd like to be your friend." He met her gaze, ripped apart at the sight of those big brown eyes brimming with unshed tears. "Before you can learn to trust others again, you need to trust your heart. What's it saying about me?"

With that loaded question, he walked from the lounge. His own heart beat fast in his chest as he made his way out to the parking lot and to his truck. Once he settled in behind the wheel, he took a deep breath, closed his eyes and leaned his head back.

When he'd told her to trust her heart, he'd been talking to himself more than anything…but now he realized it was solid advice.

Drake knew Marly was a strong woman, but someone had pushed that strength aside and had taken advantage of her. He intended to honor his promise of friendship and not press for more. Marly was special, she was worth being patient for, and Drake couldn't wait to see what happened next.

Chapter Four

What had she been thinking, agreeing to this plan? Hadn't she already mentally scolded herself for getting too close to Chief St. John? She should be steering clear of the man, yet when he'd looked at her with those mesmerizing eyes and offered compassion and support, she couldn't deny him anything.

Which was why she was now straightening her home like a maniac, picking up random toys and stray shoes while Willow ran the vacuum. Thankfully the rental home was small, so the cleanup wasn't too hard—it was more the pressure of having Drake in her home that had her nerves on edge.

The vacuum shut off and Willow wheeled it back through the hall and under the steps where the cleaning supplies were kept.

"I better get extra pizza for all that sweeping," Willow mumbled as she came back through the house.

Putting away the last of the clean dishes, Marly smiled. "I'll make sure you get extra. And maybe even dessert for all your help."

Willow's smile widened. "Like brownie delights?"

Marly shrugged. "I'm not sure if we'll make brownie delights or not, but I'm sure we can come up with something."

Climbing onto a wooden bar stool at the small center island in the kitchen, Willow rested her head in her hands. "What's the chief coming over for?"

"We're going to try to figure out a way to help Jeremy's family," Marly explained, hanging her plaid kitchen towel over the oven handle. "Medical bills can be expensive, and Jeremy will need a lot of extra special care to make sure he's all better."

"We've been making him get-well cards in class. Jeremy likes trucks, so I drew him a big red truck on my card."

Marly reached across the island and smoothed stray strands from Willow's forehead. This morning her blond mass had been tamed into two braids, but now, well, apparently recess had gotten the better of the hairdo.

A tap on the front door jerked Marly upright. Heart pounding heavily, she knew the second Drake entered her home, she'd start getting all fluttery, and the last thing she needed was her daughter picking up on any vibes. Not that a five-year-old was very in tune with adults' feelings, but Marly couldn't take the chance.

Kevin didn't need more leverage in his attempt to get full custody.

This was just an evening of acquaintances getting together to collaborate on how to make a family's life a little easier. Any feelings toward Drake that wanted to take root would have to be removed before they could grow. Any type of relationship at this point, especially with a man, was not a smart move.

When her doorbell rang again, Marly pulled herself from her thoughts. To assume Drake had feelings on his end was very presumptuous of her. Yes, he'd seemed interested, but did that mean he was going to act on anything? She was borrowing trouble when she had too much on her plate to keep her mind occupied already.

"I'll get it, Mama." Willow ran by her and headed to the front room. "Can I let in the chief?"

"Yes, and thank you for asking before letting someone in the house."

Marly smoothed a hand over her ponytail, then made sure her side bangs were covering the scar. Even though her hair was still in the same shape it had been in at work, she'd at least changed from her scrubs and put on her ever-dressy yoga capris and V-neck T-shirt. Hey, she wasn't inviting him over for anything romantic, and this was the real her. Nothing fancy, no jewelry, no makeup, plain-Jane hair.

The days of always worrying about her appearance had long since passed. And to be honest, she loved the Marly she was rediscovering.

"Wow, pizza?" Willow jumped up and down. "You're the coolest, Mr. Chief."

Marly stepped into the front room and smiled. The sight of Drake in a gray T-shirt pulled taut across his shoulders and faded jeans did nothing to help her motivational speech she'd just given herself about not having time to think of him as anything other than a friend.

How could she ignore such a visually tempting man? And the fact that he was concerned about a helpless little boy only made her heart clench more. Oh, and the way he'd handled a parking lot full of kindergarteners… Yeah, the man was fast becoming more and more appealing.

"How about you call me Drake?" he suggested to Willow.

Drake's lopsided grin and the way he ruffled her daughter's hair had Marly crossing her arms over her chest. "Thanks for bringing the pizza."

He nodded his greeting and held the pizza box in one hand while closing the door behind him with the other. "I hope you guys like fish eggs on it."

"Fish…eggs?" Willow asked, throwing a worried look to her mother, then shrugged. "I guess I'll try it."

"I'm teasing," Drake said with a laugh that showcased his wide smile and white teeth.

Darn him. Was there nothing about the man that wasn't perfect? Joking with her child and not acting as though Willow was in the way like…

No, she wasn't pulling Kevin into this evening. He occupied enough of her waking hours between the texts, voice mails and her mind working overtime on when he would start looking for them.

Right now, she just wanted a few hours of peace,

away from her monster ex and away from her own worried thoughts.

Marly shot a smile to Drake and pointed to Willow. "This kid would try anything. She's a tough one to scare."

Drake's bold eyes went back to Willow, his brows rose. "Really? A brave girl? I like that. You sound more like a firefighter than a kindergartener."

Willow beamed. "When can I take a ride on your fire truck?"

"Willow," Marly scolded. "I'm sorry. She was really impressed the other day at the field trip. She's hardly talked about anything else."

Drake moved through the living room and handed the pizza box to Marly. "I don't mind at all, actually. What kind of chief would I be if I didn't keep my promise to let such a brave girl take a ride on the truck? You may become a firefighter one day and you'll need the experience."

"Me?" Willow squeaked, jumping up and down. "A firefighter? That would be awesome!"

The man had been in the house for all of two minutes and had already captivated both women in the room, for totally different reasons.

"Come on in and eat," Marly suggested as she turned and headed toward the back of the house. "You two can discuss firefighter training over fish eggs."

Before long, paper plates were filled with chips and pizza. Marly pulled out two cans of soda and a bottle of water. They gathered around the small kitchen table and Marly resisted the urge to make everything perfect.

The man sitting across from her was nothing like the man she'd left. Nothing.

Marly highly doubted Drake cared if he ate off paper plates or fine china. He didn't seem the type to need a linen napkin over a paper towel. She refused to bow down to a man's every wish again. She would make Willow happy first, herself second, and if a man came along and could put up with being third on her list of priorities, then there was a slight chance that she would consider him in her life.

To be honest, she doubted the yearning to want another man would come for a long, long time. Yes, she found Drake attractive and had those tingles in her belly when he was around, but she wasn't ready for anything beyond that. How could she be? She was still recovering emotionally and physically from her last relationship.

"Everything okay?" Drake asked, pausing as he reached for another piece of pizza. "You wandered off for a bit."

Marly took a sip of her soda and nodded, forcing herself to be in the moment. "Just thinking. So what have you thought of for a fund-raiser?"

He slid the piece onto his plate and met her gaze. Those blue eyes could mesmerize a nun. She shoved a chip into her mouth to try to keep her mind on the task and not the man. Easier said than done when the man in question was as potent as Drake St. John.

"We need something where the town comes together," he told her, oblivious to the turmoil inside her. "The more people who pitch in, the more support Shawn and Amy will have. This isn't just about monetary needs, they need moral support and people to lean on."

Rocked by his selfless declaration, Marly nodded in agreement. "You're absolutely right. They will need assistance from all angles."

"How about a bake sale?" Willow chimed in around a mouthful of pizza. "The school had one the other day to raise money for books for the library."

"Honey—"

"Willow." Drake cut off Marly, giving her a wink. "I think a bake sale is a wonderful idea. Your mother and I were thinking of something really big for the entire town, but those people would love some treats, I'm sure."

Drake took a bite of pizza, took a full gulp of his soda before continuing, "What about something that incorporates several aspects of raising money? Maybe a dunking booth or three-legged races?"

Marly's mind started working overtime. Now, this was an aspect from her old life she was actually glad to have instilled in her. Planning, organizing a way to raise funds.

"Like a festival?" Marly asked. "That's great, Drake."

"A festival?" Willow smacked her hands on the table and jumped from her chair. "Can we have a Ferris wheel like the one we rode on a few weeks ago, Mama?"

Marly laughed. "Oh, honey. It would be quite expensive to bring in a Ferris wheel. The whole point of this would be to make money, so probably nothing like that."

As the pizza was devoured, Drake and Marly volleyed back and forth various ideas. Some were good, some not so good.

"I'll get you a pen and paper, Mama."

When Willow ran out of the room, Marly shook her head and started gathering the paper plates. "That child has more energy than I can keep up with at times."

Drake came to his feet and folded the chip bags. "Where do these go?"

"Oh, just leave them. I'll get everything." Marly tried to busy herself so she didn't have to look in his eyes, didn't have to talk about anything personal. "What do I owe you for the pizza?"

Drake rested his hands on his narrow hips and shook his head. "Absolutely nothing."

"I need to pay at least half," Marly told him, reaching for her purse on the counter.

He laid his hand over hers. She hadn't even seen him move toward her, but when she looked up and her eyes met his, she tensed. His hands were so big, totally blanketing her own. An image flashed in her mind of other large hands on her, hurting her. She forced herself not to completely seize up beneath his delicate touch.

Between that intense stare and the heat from his hand, Marly swallowed hard, trying to reinforce that pep talk she'd had with herself earlier.

Feeling anything toward Drake was a bad, bad idea.

"You owe nothing," he told her, keeping his eyes locked onto hers. "Maybe you can buy next time."

Holding her breath and praying her voice came out strong, Marly asked, "Will there be a next time?"

Before he could respond, Willow burst back into the

room. "I got paper and a pen," she yelled. "Now, spell everything slow for me and I'll make notes."

Drake's hand slid away from Marly's as she continued to stare at him. Willow was oblivious to the tension that had settled between them, but it left Marly… confused, intrigued…fascinated.

What was Drake thinking? Flirting was one thing, but the way he looked at her, as if he was attracted and ready to act on it… How could she cope with a man who wanted anything from her? She truly had nothing left in her to give. But, she vowed, she would never be this low again. She would never allow another man to break her.

Marly turned toward her daughter and concentrated on helping Willow write down some simple notes for the festival. If they were going full speed ahead with this plan, Marly feared there would most definitely be a next time she and Drake got together.

And Willow couldn't always pose as the chaperone.

What the hell had he been thinking?

Drake picked up another nail, positioned it against the two-by-four and hammered it home with more force than necessary.

"Whoa. Who are you pissed at?"

Drake glanced over his shoulder to see Eli standing in the doorway to the addition Drake was adding onto the back of his house.

"Nobody," he mumbled.

That wasn't true. He was beyond mad with himself for allowing his hormones to control his actions. He knew Marly was skittish, yet he'd still flirted, hoping to see a reaction. Her deer-in-the-headlights look when he'd placed his hand over hers was all he'd needed to know that she remained very cautious and scared.

"You're mad," Eli retorted, stepping into the room. He ran his hand along the already placed beams and glanced over the work. "Is it the mayor again?"

Drake grunted, driving in another nail. "It's never *not* the mayor."

"Something more than usual?" Eli asked.

Carefully dropping his hammer to the subfloor, Drake shook his head. "Nothing I can't handle. What are you doing here? Don't you have a clinic to run, wife to love on or baby to feed?"

Eli's smile widened. As the oldest brother, Dr. Eli St. John had been busy lately with taking over their father's clinic, marrying his high school sweetheart and becoming a father.

Nora and Eli had drifted apart when Eli had gone into the military. Nora had married Eli's best friend, but when Nora's husband was killed in action, she had discovered she was pregnant. Now that she and Eli had found their way back to each other, Drake had never seen his brother so happy.

"Actually Nora took the baby and went to visit Mom and Dad. I saw your truck when we passed by and since I hadn't seen you in a week, I told her I'd check up on you and be right back." Eli crossed his arms over his chest and leaned against a stud. "Care to tell me what's wrong?"

"Everything, actually." Walking over to the sawhorses with plywood on top for a makeshift worktable, Drake twisted off the cap of his water and downed half the bottle. "Jeremy is still recovering from that damn fire, the mayor is the bane of my existence and now Marly is consuming my thoughts."

"Marly?" Eli's brows raised. "Who's Marly?"

The St. John boys were known for being jokesters and hellions, but Drake was thankful for once that his brother didn't razz him about saying another woman's name.

"She's the nurse caring for Jeremy."

Eli continued to stare, as if weighing his words before they came out. "This is the first time you've mentioned any woman since Andrea."

Raking a hand over his head, Drake sighed and downed the last half of his water before tossing the bottle into the trash in the corner.

"I've been on a few dates," Drake commented. "Nothing has progressed beyond date one with anybody, so I never mentioned them."

"Is this nurse a serious thing?" Eli asked.

With a laugh, Drake shook his head. "She's skittish, she's a single mom to an adorable little girl and she's running from something. But as far as she and I go, we're nothing. She consumes my thoughts and I don't know if that's the protector in me wanting to know more and help her or if I'm actually attracted on a level I didn't think existed anymore."

"Wow, man." Eli sighed and walked around the spacious room that was now ready for the drywall. "I don't even know what to say. I mean, this is great that you may be finally moving on. You haven't even gone on a date with the woman and you're already torn up. It may not be serious to her, but it's turning into something for you."

"It's crazy. I barely know her, but everything in me wants to." Drake crossed his arms over his chest, twisting his neck from side to side to work out some kinks.

Holding his arms out, Eli shrugged. "Hey, I'm not judging the time frame. Just because it took me and Nora years to get it right doesn't mean you can't feel something for Marly this soon. You know Andrea would want you happy, would want you to move on."

Drake knew this in his head, but saying he could move on and actually doing it were two different things. He was much stronger than he was even a year ago thanks to his family and his therapist.

Yeah, he wasn't afraid to admit he'd had to see a shrink after Andrea passed. What man wouldn't have to deal with those demons? He'd loved Andrea with all of his heart and he'd blamed himself for so long for being unable to save her. But in the end, he knew there was nothing he or the first responders on the scene could've done.

The survivor's guilt would always be a nugget embedded deep in his heart, his mind, but Eli was right. Moving on was the only way he would conquer that nightmare. And Marly may just be the woman to help him do that…if he could get her to open up and relax around him.

"What makes you think this woman is running from

something?" Eli asked, turning back to face Drake. "Do you think it's something illegal?"

"No, nothing like that." Drake swiped his arm across his forehead to wipe away the sweat. "She's scared."

"Of you?"

His mind flashed to the second in the nurses' lounge when she'd gone pale after he'd gripped her shoulders, then again when he'd slid his hand over hers at her house.

"No, but I'm laying money some jerk has damaged her."

"So she's not from here," Eli deduced. "Is she divorced?"

Shrugging, Drake realized he didn't know too much about her personal life. He also figured Marly wasn't the type of woman who would give such information up easily, either.

"I assume so, but I'm not sure. She has a little girl."

Eli smiled. "Really, at this point, all you know is she's afraid of something, you're attracted to her and she has a kid? Yeah, sounds like your protective instincts are all over this."

Drake sank down on the bucket of plaster and rested his elbows on his knees. "I'm screwed, Eli. I've put myself in a position where I'll be seeing her fairly often, and each time I'm around her, I want to find more reasons to stick around. Maybe if she gets more used to me she'll feel safe, feel as if she can let her guard down a little."

"Do I need to call Cameron?" Eli asked, referring to

their other brother. "I mean, if we're having a Dr. Phil moment, I think it's only fair we include him."

Drake laughed. "I should've known your compassion would only last a minute before turning into sarcasm."

Eli slapped Drake on the back and settled down on the wood subfloor. "You wouldn't have me any other way."

Drake eyed his brother on the floor and laughed harder. "I'm not helping you up, old man."

Eli flipped Drake the finger. "So why the hell are you and Marly spending so much time together?"

Drake went into the details about the town festival, his harebrained idea to pull Marly in on the project and the fact that he'd found himself lingering at her house the other night.

What Drake didn't go into details about was how he'd felt the entire time he had to endure looking at her in those snug pants and T-shirt and how her bouncy ponytail had made her seem younger than he figured she was. Nor did he go into the whole saga of how fast she'd turned him inside out and twisted his insides all over the place with nerves and wants and needs.

How could he have slid down this slippery slope so fast?

At least his emotions weren't one-sided. He'd seen that pulse at the base of her neck quicken, the widening of her big brown eyes and the way she held her breath when he'd laid his hand over hers. She may have had a layer of fear masking her desire, but the passion was there nonetheless.

Chapter Five

Marly rested her hands on the edge of the counter at the nurses' station and sighed. Jeremy was going to be transported to Nashville Children's Hospital at the end of the week.

Now more than ever Shawn and Amy would need support. The fund-raiser couldn't come soon enough.

"Hey."

Marly lifted her head and blinked back tears that threatened to fall. "Drake," she greeted, trying to paste on a convincing smile.

His eyes studied her, seemed to see beyond the exterior as if he could zero in on her hurts. "Is it Jeremy? Did he take a turn for the worse?"

Marly shook her head. "No, no. He's still on the road to recovery. I just…" She trailed off and sighed as she turned to grab her purse from the desk chair. She'd laid it there moments ago and had wanted to look over one last set of patient's vitals before leaving. "I'm headed out, actually. Sorry if I worried you for no reason."

"If you're upset, I'm still worried, and there's definitely a reason."

Warmth spread through her. Beyond his physical appeal, Drake St. John truly had a hero's heart. And from the few encounters she'd had with him, she already knew he was a natural-born protector.

What did he see when he looked at her, though? Did he see the vulnerability she'd tried so hard to hide? Did he just see a single mom afraid to face each new day and the monsters that could creep up at any time and steal her happiness?

"Can you wait just a minute?" he asked. "I want to pop in to see Jeremy and then I'll walk you out. We can talk."

As much as she wanted to leave on her own, she figured if they were going to talk about the festival, this would be as good a time as any. If he wanted to talk about anything else, well, this would be the best place.

"I can wait," she told him.

She didn't wait long, but when Drake stepped from Jeremy's room, the man had that sad, lost look about him again. Something haunted him, as well.

Weren't they just a pair?

Those bright blue eyes met hers as he strode across the hall. "Ready?" he asked.

Marly nodded and waited until they exited the pediatric unit before she spoke up. "You know, if it bothers you to see Jeremy, maybe you should stop coming by every day."

Drake glanced down at her but kept walking toward the main entrance. "It doesn't upset me to see him. It makes me angry and frustrated. I've done all but tap-dance on the mayor's desk to get his attention that we need to hire the rest of my men back on the department, but he's a jerk and that's a story for another time."

The passion in his tone confirmed the man was a hero doing a hero's job and not just acting the part of a caring citizen. Drake St. John wasn't so complex. She had a feeling what you saw was what you got with him. Unlike her ex, who delighted in putting on a show for the public and turning into a monster behind closed doors.

As they exited the hospital, the late-afternoon sun greeted them, and Marly pulled her sunglasses from her purse. Before she could put them on, her cell rang. Juggling her purse on her forearm, her glasses in one hand, Marly pulled out her phone.

"One second," she told Drake as she answered without looking at the number.

"Hello."

"You've not returned my calls."

Chills crept over Marly despite the heat from the sun. "I've been busy working."

Her eyes darted to Drake, who was studying her. This was the very last thing she needed. Being humiliated in private was bad enough; she refused to bring her dirty world out in the open.

"Too busy to talk to your husband?" he scolded.

Marly turned her back on Drake. "This is not a good time."

"You'll make time for me," he ordered. "We need to talk in person. I've allowed this charade to go on long enough. I am hitting the campaign trail hard shortly and my family needs to be with me."

"We're divorced," she whispered. "We're not a family."

"We are a family, and we will present ourselves as such. I've kept this divorce from the media, but you will stand by my side during these next few months."

Like hell she would. "I'm hanging up, Kevin."

Months ago she wouldn't have cut him off and disconnected the call, but she wasn't afraid of his wrath now. No, right now she feared that he'd use his power to take Willow away. Not that he was interested in a tomboy with pigtails. He wanted a refined family, a family that would make his image spotless and win over the voters. But he would try to use Willow as a pawn, and that was something Marly refused to allow. It was only a matter of time before he'd had enough, when he realized she wasn't coming back. Then he would exhaust all resources to find her and their daughter. Marly had to be ready and on guard.

After dropping her phone into her purse and sliding on her glasses, Marly took a deep breath and turned back to Drake, who had his dark brows drawn.

"Everything okay?" he asked, taking his aviator shades from his pocket and sliding them on to cover his vibrant eyes.

"Fine," she lied.

The wind started moving her hair about and she quickly reached for her side bangs, but they'd already flopped the other way. Marly jerked them back over and turned her head, hoping he wouldn't say anything, hoping he hadn't seen the puckered, jagged scar.

"Jeremy is actually getting moved at the end of the week," she told him, steering the conversation away from anything remotely regarding the phone call or the scar she figured he'd seen. "Were you able to talk with the mayor about having the festival in the park?"

Drake groaned and started heading toward the parking lot. "The mayor and I aren't exactly on great terms right now, so I sent someone else."

"Who did you send?" Marly asked, falling into step beside him.

"My brother, Cameron. He's the police chief, so I figured the chances of us getting the park for the day we want would be greater coming from the man who would provide some security."

Keys clutched in her hand, Marly gestured toward her SUV. "This is me. So you're the fire chief, your brother is the police chief. Anybody else in your family ruling this town?"

With a chuckle, Drake opened her driver's door after she clicked the button to unlock it. "No, but we do have another brother, Eli. He's a doctor and actually took over my father's practice just a few months ago."

Marly's head was spinning. Three powerful men, all pretty much holding vital roles in the town. Were his brothers handsome and potent like Drake? Marly couldn't even imagine. Surely all the single ladies in town were beating down the doors of the St. John brothers.

"So what did your messenger brother say?" Marly asked, tossing her purse onto the passenger seat and crossing her arms to face Drake.

"The mayor was completely on board. Of course, his reelection campaign is coming up, so anything to look good for the community."

Marly quirked a brow. "I'm assuming he feels just as warm and fuzzy toward you."

Drake's smile spread across his handsome face. "We're pretty much on the same page of warm and fuzzy feelings."

"So the date and the place are all set?"

Marly really tried to focus on the project, but Drake's broad shoulders and towering height blocked the sun and gave her ample opportunity to appreciate what great shape he was in. The man did physical labor, earning his muscles the old-fashioned way as opposed to in an air-conditioned gym like her vain, pampered ex. The list of differences between the two men was adding up quickly. Odd how at first she'd considered the two so similar simply because of their size and powerful positions. Drake and Kevin were at opposite ends of the male spectrum.

"The guys at the department are all on board, too," he went on. "One guy is already drafting up some flyers and another guy was calling some area businesses to see if they'd donate some prizes for an auction."

Marly smiled. "You're really taking control of this."

Shrugging, he added, "I have to."

She wasn't sure if he was blaming himself for Jeremy's accident, but she knew guilt and sorrow when she saw it.

"None of this is your fault." She reached out, placed a hand on his biceps. The thick muscle twitched beneath her palm. "Jeremy will be okay."

"I know this isn't my fault. This accident falls on the mayor's shoulders, since he cut funding and took three good men from my department." Drake glanced down at his feet, shaking his head. "I just hate that Jeremy will lose a good chunk of his school year and he'll be emotionally scarred from the nightmares of living through a fire, and then with all these upcoming surgeries..."

Marly squeezed his arm, waiting until he looked back up at her. "He's a strong boy," she told him. "He's young and healthy. He'll recover faster than you or I would in this situation. Trust me when I say you're a hero to him."

"I was doing my job, that's all." Drake reached up, took her hand from his arm and held it between his own strong, warm hands. "You're still new to town, so you should know, hero material is the last thing that comes to mind when people here think of me. My teen years set a precedent that I can't seem to shake. I'm human. I make mistakes."

He dropped her hand abruptly, leaving a shiver that coursed through her. What else was he referring to? He realized Jeremy's accident was out of his control, but there was something else that bothered him. He'd alluded to the fact that the residents of Stonerock knew, but what? What demons chased him?

"Sorry," he muttered. "I just…hate that label. I mean, I love my job and I'm good at it. I don't need to be elevated to a status beyond that."

Only a true hero would be so humble and sincere. Those defensive walls around Marly's heart continued to crumble.

"I'll talk to the art teacher at the school and see about maybe having a painting station set up or even face painting. Even if we just charged a buck, that would really start to add up."

Drake nodded. "Perfect. Cameron even mentioned having some guys from the department doing fingerprinting of the kids to keep on file for safety."

"That's a great idea. Not that any parent wants to think of their child missing, but better to be safe, and the kids would love it."

Marly hugged her arms tighter around her waist. Her daughter may not be taken by a stranger, but there was a very good possibility she'd be taken by a justice system that could be bought for the right price. Just the idea sickened her.

"You okay?" Drake asked, taking a step closer.

Her back was still against the open door of her SUV, and she hated how her body responded to his nearness. The overpowering man should frighten her, but other than his physical appearance, there was nothing intimidating about Drake St. John. The fire chief was all heart from what she could see. He truly cared and wasn't afraid to show it. And that made him infinitely sexier.

Which made her wish she were at a different point

in her life right now where she wasn't afraid to open up and let someone in. But she simply wasn't ready.

"It's just been a long day," she told him.

"Listen, I realize we don't know each other that well, but I told you before I'm a good listener and I can be a good friend."

Oh, how she wished she could trust him. She honestly had no clue how she'd fight this battle on her own, but dare she confide in Drake, who threatened her from so many angles?

The biggest threat was the feeling that slithered through her whenever she was around him. More than anything she wanted to take him up on that friendship proposal, and perhaps she could, but there were still things she couldn't discuss with him.

Would he think her a terrible mother for taking Willow away from her father? Would he think she should've stayed married for the sake of the child?

"I'm just having an issue with my ex," she told him honestly. "Nothing I can't handle."

"That who called you earlier?" he asked, straightening his shoulders. "Is he causing problems?"

Instantly he came to her defense, and she so wanted to share her fears, her worries. He had no idea what she'd done, what her ex had done...yet he was immediately on her side.

Still, Marly had to be cautious and keep her secrets close to her heart, because she couldn't drag Drake into her world, leaving him vulnerable to Kevin's wrath, because Kevin could have Drake off the fire department in the proverbial blink of an eye. Kevin wouldn't think twice about throwing his power around to prove that he could hurt anyone in Marly's life just because he wanted to.

"No more problems than usual." She took a deep breath, pleased that she'd shared a very minor part of herself with her new friend. "I need to get home to Willow. She's expecting dinner, and she's suddenly asking about fish eggs."

A corner of Drake's mouth tipped up. "Shall I bring a specialty pizza?"

Marly laughed and realized that she'd done more of that with Drake in just the short time she'd known him than in the past several months.

"No," she replied. "I'm actually going to cook a real meal, sans fish eggs."

Part of her wanted to invite him over, but the logical side of her brain told her she'd better steer clear of temptation.

And as much as she hated to admit it, Drake St. John was becoming more and more tempting by the minute. "Can I call you later?" he asked.

Surprised, Marly jerked back. "Um…"

"To discuss the festival," he added.

"Oh, yes. I put Willow to bed at eight on school nights, so if you want to call after that I'll be free to talk."

Her bangs started to drift in the breeze again, and before she could reach up to control them, Drake's hand came up, smoothed them down and leaned in within a breath of her as he removed his sunglasses with the other hand.

"You don't have to hide your scars from me," he whispered. "I carry my own, they're just on the inside."

His eyes landed on hers and Marly could swear he could see hers through her sunglasses. Could he hear her heart pounding? Could he feel the electrifying tension that crackled between them?

"I have a feeling we'll be better friends than either of us first thought." Drake slid his glasses back on and turned to walk away. "I'll call you later," he called over his shoulder.

Marly stood staring after him until he disappeared amongst the sea of cars in the parking lot.

When she sank onto the driver's seat, she quickly started the vehicle to get some much-needed AC flowing. Drake had not asked her about her scar; he hadn't stared at it like it was the ugliest thing he'd ever seen.

No, he'd been perceptive enough to know she wanted her hair to hide the ugliness. What he didn't know was that she wanted to hide the ugliness of the situation behind the scar, but there was no hiding or blanketing the truth of her past.

She'd been the abused wife of a powerful politician, and she was about to face down the enemy. There was no way in hell she'd ever return, let alone with their impressionable daughter. She'd fight the devil himself if she had to.

Marly feared she just may have to lean on someone for support. And, so far, the only contender in the "someone" category was the mesmerizing, somewhat vulnerable, incredibly sexy fire chief.

Chapter Six

"So tell me about this woman."

Drake groaned at his sister-in-law's abrupt statement and immediately eyed his brother across the dining room table. If the table weren't so wide, Drake would've given Eli a swift kick to the shins for opening his big mouth.

"What woman?" his mother asked, her fork clanging against her plate.

Drake narrowed his gaze at his brother, who merely raised his brows and shrugged. Eli was so going to get it after family dinner.

Drake turned his attention to Nora, who merely stared at him as if she had nothing else to do but wait for his response. If he didn't love her so much, he'd give her the same death glare he'd just awarded Eli.

"Don't get too excited," he started, wiping his mouth with his napkin and easing back in the dining room chair. "I met a nurse at the hospital who is taking care of Jeremy, the little boy from the fire two weeks ago. We're working together on a fund-raiser and festival to raise money to help Shawn and Amy with the expenses."

Mac St. John rested his arms on either side of his now-empty plate. "That poor boy. How's he doing?"

Mac was the retired town doctor, but only because his own doctor recommended he slow down since having quadruple bypass just a few months ago.

"He's getting better every day," Drake replied, thankful the topic had veered off course. "He's being transported to Children's in Nashville tomorrow."

"So sad," his mother said, shaking her head. "A mother's worst nightmare is to have her child hurt or injured."

Nora nodded in agreement. "I don't know what I'll do when Amber gets hurt for the first time."

Drake smiled. His little niece was taking a nap in the other room, but Drake knew Nora and Eli were awesome parents and would be able to handle future challenges. "What about this nurse?" Nora asked, resting her elbow on the table, her chin on her palm. "Is she married?"

Drake shrugged. "We're only planning a fund-raiser, not planning a wedding shower."

He hated how irritated this topic made him. He hated that he'd told his brother something in private and now his entire family was staring at him, minus Cameron, who was away working on some hush-hush big case.

Drake was talking with a woman. So what? Just because he hadn't really associated with a woman since Andrea had passed away didn't mean anything. Drake took a drink of his sweet tea and avoided the eyes around the table staring at him. Just because his attraction for Marly had grown each time he'd been with her didn't mean he would or even could act on them. As slowly as he was moving with her, the ball was in her court.

She was scarred, visibly so, and it made him want to tear apart the man who'd laid a hand on her. No wonder she was so skittish, so cautious. If Drake were a betting man, he'd say it was her ex who had abused her.

And that alone made Drake want to be closer to her, to protect her.

Suddenly he felt sick. Had Willow been a victim, as well? Any man that laid a hand on a woman or child wasn't a man at all, but a monster. Even if Willow hadn't been a victim, she could have witnessed her mother's abuse. There was no excuse for a woman or child to go through such evil.

If Drake found out who had harmed Marly, there wouldn't be a corner of this world the man could hide.

"You're looking pretty angry there, bro."

Eli's comment jerked Drake back to reality. "Maybe that's because I told you something that was private."

"Don't blame Eli," Nora said, coming to her feet and picking up her plate. "He tells me everything. I was the one who was curious."

"I'll have to remember to confide in Cameron next

time," Drake replied with a grin. "He'd only tell his best friend, Megan, but he's even too busy to see her lately."

"I'm still worried about him," their mother said. "I know he's busy being the police chief, but he's more out of touch than usual, and he's so closed off when I do see him."

Drake had noticed and he knew Eli had, as well. In fact, they'd discussed their mother's worries with Cameron several weeks ago, but the man was deep into some operation he couldn't discuss. Drake just prayed that by the time Cameron wrapped up this case he wasn't burned out on the job.

The only person Cameron seemed to keep in close contact with lately was Megan. Cam never kept anything from her. Hopefully whatever he was battling, he was at least confiding in Megan.

"He'll be fine," Drake assured his mom as he stood, too, and started gathering plates. "Dinner was great, as always. I'm going to carry these in, and then I need to get going. I'm covering for a guy tonight for a couple hours."

"Any luck with the mayor?" his father asked.

Drake's grip on the plates tightened at just the mention of the pudgy man who sat on his butt behind a desk all day. "About as much luck as getting money to fall from the sky. He's a useless politician and is only in the position for the name and recognition. Pathetic. I only hope voters see that come election time."

"I'm sure they will," Eli chimed in. "This town is too small and he's so lazy. His lack of effort hasn't gone unnoticed."

After Drake had stacked most of the dishes in the dishwasher, he gave his mother and sister-in-law a kiss on the cheek, said farewell to his dad, who was looking much better since his surgery, and eyed Eli across the room. With a nod, he silently bid his goodbye. He was still a bit ticked that Eli would tell Nora about Marly, but he supposed if Andrea were still alive, they'd be married and Drake would tell her everything.

But she wasn't alive.

Drake slid behind the wheel of his oversize truck and headed toward the department. Soon he'd have to touch base with Cameron about the festival anyway. Drake would just use that opportunity to discuss, once again, the worry their mother had. And Drake was starting to become concerned himself.

For now, he had his own issues to deal with, and figuring out what to do with his growing feelings for Marly was starting to take top priority.

Would she even let him in? Would she trust him enough to talk? Because Drake seriously wanted to know about those scars. There was no way around it. He wanted to know what had happened, wanted to know how he could make sure she was never victimized again.

But pressing Marly for details could cause further emotional damage. Drake knew an abused woman when he saw one, and his gut clenched at the thought of anyone's hands marring her perfect, delicate skin.

As he pulled into the station, he noticed two of his guys relaxing on the bench out front. This rarely happened, which meant the downtime was more than likely the calm before the storm, especially since it was a weekend night. Drunks were sure to be out, wrecks were bound to happen and the jaws of life were always at the ready.

Drake pulled into his assigned parking spot and killed the engine just as his phone vibrated in his pocket.

Sliding it out, he smiled at the display screen.

"Marly," he answered. "What's up?"

"Drake…um…hi. I thought I'd get your voice mail."

Intrigued at her hesitancy, Drake gripped the phone. "Is everything all right?"

Marly sighed, then hesitated. "I've been thinking about that friendship thing. I think I'd like to take you up on your offer."

Drake's heart started pumping faster, and a wide grin spread across his face. She was letting him in. He figured his olive branch would be dangling a bit longer, but he was glad she'd accepted it. He was also nervous about taking this next step with a woman who gave him the first set of attraction nerves since he'd met Andrea.

"I'm glad," he told her, finding that he was more excited than scared at letting someone into his own life. "But you sound a little, I don't know, sad. You sure you're okay?"

"Yeah, I just…"

"Marly." Worry settled in, and he wondered what she was truly battling. "Are you at home?"

"I am. I've just had a bad couple of days and I called you on impulse. I'm sorry."

No way was he letting her out of the conversation now that he'd gotten her this far. "Don't be sorry for calling me." He never wanted her to be sorry for anything where he was concerned. "Isn't that what friends are for?"

Marly's soft laughter filled the phone. "I suppose. Are you busy? I was wondering if you'd like to run over. Willow and I made some cookies."

Dropping his head against the back of the seat, Drake wished now more than ever the department had more manpower so he had the time off.

"I'm actually working."

"Oh, Drake. I'm sorry I bothered you. Why didn't you say so?"

"It's no bother, I just pulled into the lot. I'm covering for one of my guys for just a few hours, but why don't I run over after if it's not too late?"

"I'm sure you'll be tired, it's okay."

Her deflated tone was definitely not okay. She'd gone out on a limb—no way in hell would he turn her away. "I'll come over. I should only be here a few hours."

"Okay. I'll try not to eat all the cookies before you get here," she joked.

Drake didn't know what had her reaching out to him of her own accord, but he didn't care. If she had the courage to step out of her comfort zone, then so did he. And maybe this was what they both needed—a good friend to share things with, to possibly tackle those demons with.

The main problem, though, was that Drake was having thoughts about Marly that had nothing to do with friendship. He had no idea why this lady, why now, but he would follow her lead and figure out the rest later.

Chapter Seven

Marly was almost grateful that he hadn't shown. It was after nine and Willow had gone to bed an hour ago. After playing in her tree house all day, then baking cookies and watching a movie, Willow had fallen into Marly's bed with her cowgirl boots still on.

They'd had a really fun day, despite the fact Kevin had called again and threatened to show up at the door.

Marly learned quickly to return those threats, because anything that would tarnish his public appeal terrified him. All she had to do was threaten to have the local paper on standby and the man backed down…a little. But still, that was enough to give her the courage and the upper hand she'd lacked during their marriage.

She'd lived in fear too long, and she refused to do it

anymore. There was no way she'd raise her daughter to fear men or feel inferior.

A soft tap on the screen door jerked Marly from her thoughts. Instantly her heart pounded, and she prayed the visitor was Drake and not Kevin making good on his threat.

Padding barefoot to the front door, Marly glanced out the window to see Drake's big black truck in the driveway. A sliver of excitement and nervousness settled deep within her. She'd reached out to him after a moment of fear and panic, and now, well, she was glad she had. Being alone with a child was scary during the best of times. She needed a friend, and surprisingly, this powerful, strong man made her feel safe.

Marly flipped the lock and opened the door. "Hey," she said with a smile. "Come on in."

"I'm sorry. I just realized what time it is." Drake remained beneath the porch lights, making no move to enter. "I can come back tomorrow."

But her nerve might be gone tomorrow. "No, really, come on in."

She stepped back and allowed him to pass. And just as he did, she inhaled that masculine, woodsy scent that seemed to always envelop her when he was around.

"We got called out to an accident or I would've been here sooner," he explained.

Marly locked the door and turned to face him. "Don't apologize for doing your job. I hope it wasn't bad."

"Bad enough." Drake shook his head and sighed. "I believe I was promised some homemade cookies?"

Marly smiled, not pressing the wreck issue. She totally understood bad days at work. Unfortunately the bad days for a nurse and a firefighter usually meant someone died or was critically injured. No point in repeating the story and reliving the trauma.

"Why don't you have a seat," she told him, gesturing to the living area. "I'll bring you some."

A weary smile spread across his face. "You're going to spoil me."

Shrugging, Marly replied, "That's what friends are for, right?"

With a heart-stopping wink, Drake nodded. "Now you're getting it."

As he sank onto her secondhand sofa, Marly went into the kitchen and put several cookies on a plate and poured Drake a glass of milk. When she stepped back into the living room, she froze.

He had his head tipped back against her sofa, his large frame took up one entire cushion and those shoulders... Oh, my. The man was breathtaking, and she needed to remember that he'd offered friendship, which was the only thing she needed right now. But that didn't mean she couldn't take a visual sampling when the moment presented itself.

He lifted his head, caught her staring and lifted a brow. "You all right?"

Shaking off her thoughts—and her fears—Marly set the plate and glass on the coffee table. "I'm fine. Just not used to seeing a man on my couch, that's all."

She sat on the chair adjacent to him and tucked her legs up onto the seat beside her. Drake dug into the cookies and milk, and in no time they were gone.

"I take it they were good," she joked.

Smiling, Drake settled back onto the couch. "Home-made cookies are my weakness. My guys and I cook at the department, but it's just not the same. We can manage basic meals, but when we venture into the baking category, it's pretty bad."

"It's just following a recipe," she told him.

With a laugh, Drake shook his head. "Yeah, but the guys I work with would rather just throw stuff together without looking at directions. It never turns out edible."

He leaned forward and raked a hand over his head. "Like this one time, one of the guys wanted to make peanut-butter cookies. We were out of peanut butter so he used jelly."

Marly laughed. "Seriously?"

"You'd have to know Tyler. He can justify anything."

Marly listened to Drake's stories of his coworkers and found herself laughing more than she had in years. When she yawned, she slapped a hand over her mouth.

"Sorry." She forced back another yawn. "That's rude of me."

Drake glanced at his watch. "No, I'm sorry. I'm rambling on and on and you probably have to work tomorrow."

"Actually, I'm off."

Drake came to his feet and picked up his plate and glass. "I didn't mean to overstay."

"Don't be silly. I enjoyed talking with another adult who isn't a coworker." She reached for the dishes. "I can take those."

Maneuvering around her, Drake headed toward the

kitchen. "I can carry my own things to the sink. You've done enough for me."

Marly leaned against the door frame separating the kitchen and living area. She didn't mean to stare, but she'd never experienced a man picking up after himself. Then again, she'd never experienced a man like Drake St. John before.

When he turned back to her, the tension in the air crackled as his eyes landed on hers. Slowly, his long strides covered the ground between them. When he stood directly in front of her, Marly knew the fun atmosphere from the living room had vanished. They'd reached the point of the evening where it was time to say goodbye, which could turn awkward really fast... unless someone took charge. And she had a feeling that take-charge person was about to show his hand.

"I'm glad you called me," he stated, his tone low. "I had a good time."

"Me, too."

Heat radiated from his body. Marly noted navy flecks in his blue eyes and spotted a tiny scar she hadn't noticed before right on the edge of his eyebrow.

"I didn't give you a chance to say much." He rested a hand just beside her head on the wall. "Did you want to talk about anything particular?"

Marly shook her head. "Not really. I prefer laughing to dredging up my problems."

His fingertip came up, slid across her forehead, along the edge of her side bangs. "Problems that have something to do with this?"

Swallowing fear that was never too far away, Marly

nodded and resisted the urge to back away so he couldn't feel her imperfection. "Yes," she whispered.

His fingertip lingered on the side of her face. "And are these problems still a threat?"

Closing her eyes, Marly nodded. She wished they weren't, but she had to be realistic. She and Kevin shared a child and there was no way he would give up his family for good, not with the image he'd portrayed to the public.

"Marly." Drake tipped her chin up with his forefinger, taking his thumb and caressing the side of her jaw. "You know you don't have to live in fear, right? I can help."

Warming at the idea of just how simple Drake made the solution sound, Marly shook her head. "I wish you could. Honestly, I wish anybody could. But this is something I have to figure out on my own. I just need a friend, someone to get advice from. Nobody at work knows about my personal life and Willow is too young to know what all is going on. I don't want her afraid."

"No child should be afraid," he stated, his eyes leveling hers. "What can I do to help?"

Marly wanted to cry at his selfless gesture, his sincere worry. "You're helping more than you know. Just having someone I can talk to, someone who doesn't have a hidden agenda means so much to me."

Drake brought his free hand up to cup the side of her face. "I might have a slight agenda," he whispered as he closed the space between them. "If you want me to stop, you should say something."

Desire coursed through her as she remained silent and tipped her head up to meet his.

Drake's lips slid over hers, softly, gently. Marly fisted her hands at her sides, afraid if she reached for him, she may yearn for more than she was ready for.

Coaxing her mouth open, Drake angled his head the opposite way and slid one arm around her waist. One hand flattened against the small of her back and the other hand traveled around to the nape of her neck. He stepped closer to her, fitting her body perfectly against his.

That solid chest against hers felt so safe, so protective. Marly let herself feel, let herself get lost in the moment, in the man.

Drake nipped at her bottom lip a second before he eased back. Those dark eyes leveled hers.

"I've wanted to do that for two weeks," he murmured, resting his forehead against hers.

Between his declaration and those protective hands still molded to her, Marly trembled. "I have, too, but I've been afraid."

Drake shifted, easing back just enough to bring his hands up to frame her face. Those rough, calloused palms slid against her cheeks as he forced her gaze to remain on his.

"You won't be afraid as long as I'm here," he promised. "Tell me what you're up against. I can't help if I don't know."

Pulling away from his comforting touch, Marly shook her head. "I can't, Drake. I know you don't understand, but trust me when I tell you that it's best you don't get involved with my problems. Or me."

Crossing her arms over her chest, Marly waited for him to reply. Silence settled heavily between them, the soft ticking of the kitchen clock the only thing breaking the strained quiet.

Marly didn't miss the way his jaw was clenched, the way his hands fisted at his sides. That familiar thread of fear slid through her, and she moved back a couple steps.

"Don't." He shook his head, raked a hand through his hair and sighed before focusing back on her. "Don't look at me like that and don't step away from me."

"You're angry," she stated, lifting her chin. "I can't deal with that. I won't deal with it."

"I'm not angry at you, Marly." Drake threw his hands up, palms out. "These hands may have gotten into fights, and if you stick around long enough I'm sure you'll hear the tales of the St. John boys. But I've never, nor will I ever, use them in a harmful way toward a woman. Ever."

"We haven't known each other very long, but I believe you." Surprisingly, she did. "But I can't get beyond the fact I lived in fear for so long. I can't, Drake. I just can't let you in."

And that was something she hadn't anticipated. When she'd left Kevin, taking only her meager savings and Willow, Marly had never dreamed she'd find a man who made her want things, who made her passion come to the surface.

"I hate him," Drake said between clenched teeth.

"Whatever bastard put that look of fear in your eyes, I hate him."

Well, that made two of them, but she refused to give Drake any further details of who her ex was. Kevin could ruin Drake's career if he ever even thought Drake was coming around Marly.

Hugging her midsection, Marly glanced at her socked feet, then back up to Drake. "I'm sorry."

"What the hell for?"

"Leading you on. Kissing you."

With slow, easy strides, he closed the distance between them. "Baby, I'm not sorry at all. Kissing you was amazing, and you'll never know how much opening up to you helped me. You're not the only one with demons, but I've conquered mine. I just want to help with yours."

He had demons. She'd assumed as much. Of course a big, strong man like Drake had conquered his demons; he seemed in control of absolutely everything.

"Nothing can be done for mine," she whispered.

Drake slid her side bangs aside, his fingertips tickling her heated skin around her scar. "Something can be done, Marly. I'm not going anywhere, and when you want help, all you have to do is ask. I won't pry. I won't make you relive all the details. But I'm not afraid to battle your demons for you."

He laid a very tender, very brief kiss on her lips, stepped around her and let himself quietly out the front door.

Marly sank against the door frame that led to the hallway, her hand covering her trembling lips.

I'm not afraid to battle your demons for you.

Tears pricked her eyes. What man would say such things? What man would step in front of a woman and slay the past that threatened her future?

A man that wanted more from the woman than she was ready to give. What would he expect from her? If she could try at any type of relationship, she would try with Drake. But right now, friendship was even stretching it.

Swiping at her damp cheeks, Marly locked the dead bolt, turned off the lights and headed to her bed. Her sweet baby still lay at an odd angle across the bed, dressed in her horse nightgown and cowgirl boots.

Moonlight slanted through the window and cut across Willow's precious face. That right there was the reason Marly couldn't get involved with anyone. Not only would Kevin tear any man apart who tried to enter Marly's life, he would also use any means to steal Willow. Marly refused to allow her daughter to be a bargaining chip.

If Marly tried to move on and have another relationship, Kevin would surely use that as a weapon in his fight to get Willow. He'd twist the scenario to say Marly was unfit, or showcase her as a woman who brought men in and out of their daughter's life. He wouldn't care that Drake was a good friend. Kevin would spin their relationship into something ugly.

Marly had to put her own needs aside, no matter how much Drake made her realize there was more to men than evil and hatred. For the first time, Drake made her feel like a desired, passionate woman.

Unfortunately fate had other plans for her future, and Drake couldn't be part of them.

Chapter Eight

Jeremy had been transported yesterday, and Marly had already received an update from the children's hospital. Jeremy was all settled in, and the doctors would begin his first surgery as soon as next week.

Marly had just finished her break and stepped out of the nurses' lounge to see a huge smile on her co-worker's face.

"What?" Marly asked, figuring she had mayo on the side of her face or something equally as embarrassing.

"You have an admirer." Lori pointed to the colorful bouquet in a short glass vase that rested on the counter. "Apparently the fire chief wasn't here just to see our patient."

Marly eyed the card sticking out of the arrangement.

As she neared, she could make out the handwritten words.

Because we're friends
D

Even though her stomach was doing a nervous dance, Marly smiled as she turned to Lori. "He's a nice man. We're working on a fund-raiser to help raise money for Jeremy's family."

Lori sat down at the desk and typed in her password to log in. "Oh, Drake is a nice man, all right. But trust me, if he's showing attention toward you, and flowers are certainly attention, he's interested."

Yeah, Marly knew how interested he was. Her lips still tingled from the night before. The places on her body where his hands had been were now cold. He'd touched areas so deep within her she wondered if she'd ever recover. And all he'd done was kiss her.

Not only was she getting in deeper than she wanted to go, she was getting in deeper than she even thought possible.

"Good for him," Lori went on as she typed notes into the computer. "After Andrea was killed I wondered if he'd find happiness again."

That shocked Marly out of her own pity party.

"Who's Andrea?" *And how was she killed?*

Lori's hands froze on the keyboard, and she threw a glance over her shoulder. "He hasn't told you about Andrea? I forget you're not from here. Andrea was his fiancée. She was killed in a car accident over a year ago."

"What?" Marly gripped the edge of the other desk chair. "That's terrible."

A fiancée? No wonder he'd mentioned he had his own demons. He'd loved someone enough to want to spend his life with her and he'd lost her. A man like Drake would love with his whole heart, would die in someone else's place...especially those he loved.

Marly couldn't imagine what losing Andrea must have felt like. The only person who held such a high value in her life was Willow. Life without her would be unbearable.

Lori went back to typing. "Those St. John boys were always raising a ruckus as teens, but they've really grown into remarkable men."

Marly had yet to meet the other two brothers, but she was starting to get the impression the men were very close...and very potent.

"I keep hearing how they were hellions," Marly joked. "Were they that bad?"

"Oh, yeah. The irony of the positions they're in now is quite hysterical. Their father was the town doctor, and that poor man was always getting calls at his clinic." Lori laughed, typed a bit more and shook her head, causing the loose bun at the nape of her neck to wobble. "One time the boys stole a police cruiser and picked up a couple other friends from school. They claimed they were doing a public service by giving their friends better drop-off service than the school bus."

Marly smiled. She could only imagine the shenanigans three teen boys had gotten into. Their poor mother.

An alarm went off in one of the patients' rooms and Marly held up her hand. "I'll get it."

The rest of the day went by in a blur, and by the time she'd gathered her things—and her gorgeous bouquet—and headed toward home, she was flat-out exhausted.

Willow would be getting off the bus about five minutes after Marly got home, so there was no time for relaxing. Which was fine. She'd relaxed enough during her years of marriage when Kevin would insist on her going to the finest salons, getting facials and massages. All so he could brag about pampering his wife.

So being a single mom and being exhausted wasn't necessarily a bad thing.

Marly had just adjusted the beautiful flowers on the small kitchen table when she heard the bus pull up out front. Sometimes Willow would get dropped off at the sitter's, other times at home. The change in scheduling didn't seem to bother Willow, and she was adjusting remarkably well to living here.

Marly had never truly told her why they'd left, only that they were taking an adventure and Daddy couldn't come. Willow would ask about Kevin, but Marly would just say how he was busy with work and, because Kevin never put Willow ahead of work, that explanation seemed to pacify her. A shame, honestly, that being without a parent didn't seem to faze a little girl when she was at such an impressionable age.

Just then the front door burst open, and Willow tossed her backpack and lunch box aside. "This was the coolest day ever!"

Marly waited, always eager to hear how her daughter's day had gone. Luckily, Willow was always having "the best day." She loved school, loved her friends, freeing Marly of some of the guilt from upending her daughter's life.

"What happened?" Marly asked.

Willow shoved her wayward hair from her eyes. The once-adorable—okay, still adorable—pigtails were now slipping down from their place. "Chief Drake came to the school with another fireman, I don't remember his name." Willow put her hands on her hips and smiled. "And Chief Drake picked me out of all the kids in the entire kindergarten. He had me come up on stage in the gym and he said I had won the fire-poster contest."

"Oh, honey." Marly held her arms open and Willow launched into her hold. "That's wonderful. Is this the poster you told me you painted in art class?"

Willow eased back and nodded, sending more hair into her little face. "Yup. And Chief Drake said it was awesome and he was proud of me."

Marly listened as Willow went on and on about how cool the chief was and when could they go to the fire department for that ride she'd been promised and could he come over again and help prepare for the festival?

Such innocence, such excitement. Marly would love to have Drake over, would love to have Drake kiss her, touch her again.

She honestly couldn't remember a time when she'd been kissed so tenderly yet so passionately. Here she was, a twenty-six-year-old woman, divorced, with a child, and she couldn't recall being kissed from someone who actually cared about her.

That was just one of the many changes she was making in her new life. From now on, she would hold herself at a higher standard, expecting to be cared for by anyone who entered her life. She deserved nothing less.

Drake and Eli were just stepping out of the local pizza place when Marly and Willow came up the sidewalk. Drake clutched the boxes and stopped, experiencing that instant kick to the gut he always got when he was around her.

"What are you doing?" Eli complained, running into his back. "I nearly dropped the wings, dude."

Marly's eyes came up to meet his, and a slow smile spread across her face. "Drake," she said as she closed the space between them. "I see we're all on the same page with dinner."

"You're Marly?" Eli asked behind him.

Drake wanted to kick his brother in the jewels. Why ask like that? Why make it sound as if Drake had been chatting up Marly to him like some high school teen who had a crush?

"I am." Her smile widened as she took her daughter's hand. "And this is my daughter, Willow."

His brother moved around beside Drake, bent down and smiled. "I'm Eli," he told Willow. "It's nice to meet you."

"Are you a fireman, too?" she asked, her eyes wide and hopeful.

"No, I'm a doctor."

The little girl's brows drew in. "You give shots?"

Eli laughed, straightening to his full height. "Sometimes, but only so people can feel better."

"Um…thanks," Marly chimed in, her eyes only on Drake. "You know, for the flowers."

"Flowers?" Eli muttered.

Careful to keep hold of the pizza boxes, Drake rammed his elbow into his brother's side. Pleased when a burst of air expelled from Eli, Drake smiled at Marly.

"You're welcome."

Marly grinned, apparently not missing a thing. "Well, we won't keep you. I promised Willow we could eat inside tonight."

"Why don't you come back with us?" Drake asked before he could stop himself, though now that the invitation was out in the open, he wasn't sorry he'd asked. "We ordered plenty and we're just going to Eli's house to watch a game."

Marly shook her head. "I couldn't do that to you guys."

"My wife won't mind," Eli added. "She'd probably love to have female company."

"Please, Mama." Willow tugged on her mother's hand. "Let's go, and I can watch the game, too."

Marly laughed. "She loves football."

Drake smiled and looked down at Willow. "What do you say to some fish-egg pizza and a game?"

Willow's smile spread across her face. "Are you teasing me again, Chief?"

Loving that little girl's infectious smile, Drake shrugged. "You'll never know unless you come over."

Willow turned those bright blue eyes up to her mother. "Can we? Please?"

Marly looked between her daughter and Drake. With a sigh, she nodded. "It looks like I'm outnumbered. Are you sure your wife won't mind?"

"I'm positive," Eli told her. "Just follow us. I don't live far."

As Marly and Willow settled back into their car, Drake and Eli piled into Eli's truck. Drake knew what was coming. Knew there was no way in hell during these next few miles that Eli wouldn't give him hell.

"So…flowers."

Drake set the bag of wings on top of the pizza boxes and fastened his seat belt. "Shut up."

"Just making a statement."

"Keep your statements to yourself."

Bringing the engine to life, Eli backed out of the parking lot. "She's pretty. Little girl is adorable, too. You ready for a family?"

Drake held on to the food and glanced in the rearview mirror to make sure Marly was back there. "I'm not getting a family, Eli."

"You haven't dated much since Andrea's death, you sent this beautiful nurse flowers, you've been to her house and you are obviously taken by that little girl. Sounds as though you're gearing up for a family to me."

Maybe so, but no way Drake would admit it aloud. After Andrea's death, he never thought he'd be ready to commit to another woman. He'd sworn she was it for him, and he could never even look at another woman with such emotions.

While he didn't have any thoughts of marrying Marly, he couldn't deny the strong pull, the intensity of his feelings and the anticipation of seeing where their relationship led them.

He may have not planned for another woman to impact his life, but he couldn't deny that Marly had sucker punched him in the gut with her beauty, her innocence and her vulnerability. No way in hell was he letting go of something that was building just because he was scared of taking another step into relationship territory.

Marly may just be the woman who had been placed into his life to help him get over that last hurdle he'd been afraid to face. Maybe this was the start of something he'd dreamed of, everything he'd wanted and never thought he'd have after Andrea.

Chapter Nine

At first Marly had wondered what on earth she'd been thinking agreeing to this, but after she and Willow had arrived at Eli's home, she realized it was a good idea.

After kissing Drake, wanting more and then pushing him away, the presence of other adults really lessened the awkwardness between them. Well, Drake may not feel awkward, but she sure did. Not a bad awkward, just…awkward. She didn't know what move to make or what he'd do next.

Being attracted to someone, knowing he felt the same way, was all new territory for her. Yes, when she and Kevin had first started dating and then gotten engaged, they had a level of attraction; she wouldn't have married him had there been no spark.

But the intensity with which Marly yearned for more

time, more kissing from Drake was beyond anything she'd ever experienced.

And now she had another layer of Drake St. John to consider. The man may be all strength and power, but he had a vulnerability that he held close to his heart. Losing a fiancée was unfathomable, and the fact Drake had been able to move on, pushing through what had to have broken him, only made her more aware of what a remarkable man he truly was.

"Sorry about that." Eli's wife, Nora, came back out onto the enclosed patio with a monitor in hand. "Had to get Amber down for her afternoon nap."

Marly smiled. "I understand. Too bad adults can't grab those afternoon naps."

Nora laughed, taking a seat on the floral-cushioned wicker chair. "So you're fairly new in town. What do you think of Stonerock?"

"I really like it," Marly answered honestly. "I wanted a small town and I wanted a nice school for Willow. We're both really happy."

That sounded convincing…didn't it?

"Where are you from?"

Marly slid her thumb over the condensation on her cup of lemonade, trying to figure out how much to reveal and still sound like a normal single mom just looking for a fresh start.

"Nashville."

"Oh, I love Nashville." Nora rested her elbow on the edge of her wicker chair and propped her head on her fist. "Were you a nurse there, as well?"

"For a few years. After I had Willow, I took time off to stay home and be with her."

Mainly because Kevin had threatened to have her fired if she didn't because he didn't want his wife working. That would look as if he couldn't take care of her financially, and image was everything after all.

"I'm so glad I'm taking a few months off to be with Amber," Nora stated. "Eli doesn't care if I return to work or not, but I love my clinic. Not that it matters. If I closed my office, my patients would just come here."

"You'd mentioned earlier being a vet. Do you love that?"

Nora nodded. "Every day is something different."

Marly took a drink of her lemonade, the tangy liquid reminding her of simple summers, and she was sorry that this one would be coming to an end soon.

"How long have you been divorced?"

Marly nearly choked on her drink at Nora's innocent question.

"I'm sorry," Nora said over Marly's coughing. "That was rude. I just assumed you'd been married and I shouldn't have done that. I was married before, but my husband was killed in the service. I hate when people assume."

Nora's backpedaling and apology gave Marly enough time to compose herself. "No, no. It's okay. I am divorced. I've been single about six months."

Longer than that, considering the loveless marriage. She'd raised Willow totally on her own, but there was no way Marly was getting into that.

"Well, you have one adorable little girl," Nora stated. "She really does love football, doesn't she?"

Marly nodded. "She does. Most people think she's this sweet, princess-type little girl with her blond hair and blue eyes. She really fools them when they realize she's a dirt-and-mud type of girl who loves sports and trucks."

"I love that you allow her to be her own person." Nora stroked the cat that had climbed up onto her lap. "So many parents try to mold their children into something they're just not meant to be."

Images of Kevin yelling about Willow's free spirit and blaming Marly played in her head. It was during one of those fights that he'd put that scar on her chin.

"Are you okay?"

Marly glanced across the patio to meet Nora's worried face. "Oh, yes. Just thinking. It is a shame when parents don't let their kids develop in their own way."

Shouting from the living room erupted, and seconds later the baby monitor lit up as the cries from Amber came through.

Nora groaned. "I've told him again and again he needs to tone it down during the games. He wakes Amber up every time there's an afternoon game."

Marly came to her feet. "Would you like me to go get her?"

"Oh, no. I'll go get her and take her to her daddy. He needs to be reminded what happens when you wake the baby," Nora smirked. "Be right back."

Marly sank back down on the wicker sofa and sighed.

This was what a family should be like. Give and take, good times with friends in a simple, loving atmosphere.

Before her parents had passed, she'd had that. Perhaps that was why she'd been so quick to marry Kevin. Marly had dreamed of raising her own family, mimicking the love and laughter she'd always known. Yet somehow she'd been blinded by a charming man with a dream for power who'd wanted her by his side. In theory it had all sounded so romantic… In reality it was a living hell.

One day at a time, she was crawling back to the life she'd envisioned for herself. And one day, perhaps she'd find her own happiness.

Drake stepped out onto the patio where Marly was obviously lost in thought. She stared straight ahead into the fenced backyard. Her legs were crossed and she absently toyed with her empty cup, spinning it slowly between her hands.

"Care if I hide here with you?" he asked, coming to sit beside her on the small sofa.

Her gaze jerked to his. "I didn't hear you come out. Um…sure."

"We woke the baby, so now Eli is being punished."

Marly straightened. "He's the baby's father, too. Is it just the mother's job to take care of the child?"

Drake held up his hands. "Whoa, I didn't mean that. I just meant because he woke Amber he would have to get her back to sleep."

Marly eased back against the floral cushion. "I'm sorry. I didn't mean to jump all over you."

"Never apologize to me," he told her. "You have nothing to be sorry for."

Her reaction told him everything he needed to know about the type of man Willow's father was. *Deadbeat dad* came to mind instantly.

"Aren't you watching the game?" she asked.

"It's halftime. Eli brought in Amber, and Willow was all excited about the baby, so she wanted to stay with them."

"Is she in the way?" Marly asked, her eyes wide. "We can go. I don't want to overstay our welcome."

Drake reached out, placing a hand on her knee. "You're not overstaying, and Willow is never in the way."

Marly's eyes held his for a second before she nodded. "Thanks."

He figured the kiss was still on her mind, which was right where he wanted it to stay, so he didn't bring it up. He wanted her to think about it, think about them. He sure as hell was.

So instead of bringing up the proverbial elephant in the room, he kept to a safer topic. As much as he wanted to dig deeper into her feelings, he also wanted to keep that line of friendship open.

"I have several items for the silent auction," he told her, pleased when she smiled. "I also rented a dunking booth, and the company was all too eager to let us rent it for half price."

"Oh, Drake, that's great." She shifted in her seat to face him fully. "I emailed the art teacher, and she was happy to have her high school class set up a face-painting station. A church in town actually contacted me about a bake sale."

"I'm picking up the flyers on Monday, and I'll bring some by your house when my shift ends. I think most people know by now, but it won't hurt to post some around town."

Marly tucked her hair behind her ear and reached to smooth her bangs. He had no doubt she did the gesture out of habit now. Every time he saw her trying to hide that scar, a new level of rage rolled through him. It absolutely sickened him to think of everything she'd endured…everything she still kept bottled inside.

"I'm excited," she told him. "I just know this will really help Shawn and Amy."

Unable to resist, Drake slid his arm across the back of the wicker love seat and toyed with the ends of her silky hair. "And what about you? What would help you?"

Marly tilted her head. "Drake, you've got to stop. You make this so hard for me."

"This what?" he asked, rubbing those golden strands between his fingertips.

A sigh shuddered through her as her eyes met his. "You make me feel things," she whispered. "I can't let this go beyond friendship."

"But you want to." He grazed the back of his knuckles down her delicate cheek. "I'm not trying to make this harder on you, Marly, but you have to know that it's been so long since I've felt anything for a woman. I can't ignore this."

Marly reached up and held on to his hand. "How long has Andrea been gone?"

Drake froze. Hearing his late fiancée's name on Marly's lips had his past and present colliding right in front of him.

"It's a small town," he told her, bringing their hands to drop into her lap. "I'm surprised you didn't hear about this before now."

Marly offered a smile. "We both have our own issues, Drake. I realize you're moving past yours, but my issues… They could destroy peoples' lives."

The reality of her words settled in and he shifted closer. "Are you trying to protect me?"

"You don't know what you'd be up against. Trust me."

The haunted look in her eyes, the sad tone of her voice had his blood boiling all over again. He'd climb these damn walls she'd erected and prove to her that real men didn't use their power to control women.

"Marly, I'm not afraid of anybody or anything." She started to look down, but he took both hands, cupped her face and forced her to look at him. "I don't know what kind of man you're used to, but I'm not a coward, and I stand up for people I care about."

Unshed tears sprang to her eyes. "He has the power to crush your career and take my daughter," she whispered. "Please, don't do this to me, to yourself."

Drake ignored her plea and closed the narrow space between them. Her mouth instantly opened to his, proving she wasn't speaking from her heart. Her heart was in this kiss, this moment. She'd become like a drug to him. The more he had, the more he craved. His hands slid into her hair, but she pulled away and came to her feet, turning her back on him.

"I won't do this to you," she whispered. "Don't ask me to."

And then she was gone. Drake sat on the sofa, wondering what the hell he could do to make her understand that he wasn't going anywhere, that he wanted to help her.

Beyond that, beyond the fact that he wanted to protect her, he had a feeling deep in his soul that Marly was a woman he could quite possibly fall in love with.

Was he ready to step into that type of commitment again? Could he open his heart fully and trust it not to be broken?

Chapter Ten

Two days later and Drake couldn't get Marly's haunting words from his mind. She was utterly convinced that if she started something with him, her ex would take action. He knew Marly was worried not only for herself, but also for Willow. Didn't she see that he wouldn't let anyone hurt them? Regardless of what happened between Drake and Marly, he refused to see any woman treated poorly, especially by someone who claimed to care for her. Drake refused to back down, and he refused to let Marly throw in the towel and give up on a life for herself.

If she'd said she wasn't interested, if she hadn't responded so passionately to his kisses, then he would back off. But Marly was just as interested as he was, and he would damn well find a way to get over this hurdle she'd placed between them.

Drake climbed the steps to the courthouse and welcomed the cool air-conditioning as he stepped into the marble, two-story entryway.

As if his mood wasn't crappy enough because of Marly's ex—a man he'd never even met—now Drake had to go meet with Mayor Butterball for a performance review. These were always a treat.

Bypassing the elevator, Drake took the steps and headed toward the mayor's office. Betty typed away at her computer, but looked up and offered a sweet smile when Drake entered.

How such a kind older woman could work for a man like Mayor Tipton was beyond him. The pay couldn't be good enough to put up with the lazy jerk.

"Chief," she greeted. "Go right on in. He's expecting you."

Goody.

"Thank you, Betty," he replied with a smile of his own.

Without knocking, Drake charged right in and closed the door behind him.

"Chief. Right on time."

Drake grunted as he took a seat in the worn leather chair. No extra words were necessary. Drake wasn't here to make friends, he was here to get this yearly review over with so he could head home and work more on his renovations. His ultimate stress reliever was pounding on two-by-fours and getting dirty and sweaty while blaring his music.

The mayor slid a folder across his desk and flipped it open. He pretended to be reading through the papers, but Drake knew full well the man had already looked over this stuff. He made it a point to be in Drake's business...and not just because he was the mayor and that was his job.

"Looks as though there was a problem at the Shack," he said without looking up.

Drake sighed. He knew this was coming. "This is the third time that restaurant has had an electrical issue. If they can't keep their box up to code, they can't stay open."

Tipton dropped the paper and glanced up. "That's the only place that the church crowd goes on Sundays. You can't keep closing them and fining them."

Drake eased forward in his chair. "Are you kidding me? Do you want a fire? Because I assure you, that will close them a hell of a lot longer."

"The Prestons are an older couple, Chief. They can't afford to lose the business."

"They can't afford to have their business burn to the ground, either." Drake's blood started pumping, as it always did around this moron. "I will continue to inspect them until I'm comfortable with their security."

Sighing, Mayor Tipton flipped the top paper over. "I also have a complaint from Helen Reed about one of your engines leaving a rut in her yard."

Drake laughed, shaking his head. "Seriously? She calls at least once a week because that damn cat of hers won't come out of the tree."

So embarrassing. He hated the stereotypical image

of a fireman getting the cat out of a tree, but the woman was nearing ninety and there was no way Drake could tell her no…even if she did complain.

"Be that as it may, you need to be more careful."

Drake clenched his fists, but said nothing. This "review" couldn't be over fast enough.

"I've also gone over the budget again for the next quarter, and I'm afraid we'll have to cut back one more man in your department."

Oh, hell no. Drake shot out of his chair.

"You've already pulled three," he retorted. "We're short staffed as it is. This is getting ridiculous."

"If the money isn't there, then there's nothing I can do."

Drake braced his hands on the desk and leaned in. "You could start cutting some of the hours of other city workers. You could start knocking off an hour from each employee in this building, and that would pay for one of my hardworking men to keep his job."

"I can't affect the lives of that many people," the Mayor defended. "It's easier to just remove one."

"Easier?" Drake laughed in disbelief. "You're all about easier. You sit behind this desk and dole out orders when you know absolutely nothing about what's going on in the town you supposedly care so much about."

"Watch it, Chief. You're treading a fine line."

Drake pushed off the desk, propped his hands on his hips and stared down at the man who had become the bane of his existence.

"I don't care about that line, *Mayor*, I care about the people who I took an oath to protect. I care about the men who work under me, who put their lives on the line every single day with little or no recognition." Drake's anger fueled his words and he couldn't stop. "What I don't care about is a lazy man who tries to play God and is more worried about image than people. And I sure as hell don't care about making your job easier. I will not sacrifice another of my men."

"Fine." The mayor pushed from his desk and came to his feet. "Consider yourself suspended without pay until further notice."

Stunned, Drake sank back on his heels. "You're not serious."

The smirk across Mayor Tipton's face had Drake resisting the urge to jump over that desk. The last thing he wanted was for his own brother to have to come arrest him.

"Oh, I'm very serious. Since you refuse to release one of your other men, you can be the one to go." The mayor picked up the file and tapped the edge of it against his desk. "I'll discuss your review with city council and we will take it from there."

"You do that," Drake said. "But I will be at that meeting. I will get my position back, and you won't be able to do a damn thing about it. Do you want to know why? Because you won't get reelected. I'll make sure of it."

Tipton's eyes narrowed. "Is that a threat?"

"It's whatever the hell you want it to be." Unable to resist, Drake swept his hand across the desk, sending papers flying. "Have a good day."

Pleased that he'd held his rage in check for the most

part, Drake stormed out of the office, the door slamming back against the wall.

He'd never been suspended before in his life. And suspended without pay? Whatever. He had a good chunk in savings, and at least his men would be able to hold on to their positions a bit longer.

But this sucked.

On the bright side? Now he had more time to devote to a certain blond nurse, and he intended to start right away.

Marly had just put brownies in the oven when her doorbell rang.

"Can I get it, Mama?" Willow called from her bedroom.

Fear settled in Marly's stomach. She'd had another threatening text from Kevin earlier, claiming he would find her if she didn't come back to him within a week. She knew he would make good on his threat.

"No, honey," Marly called back. "I've got it."

She'd been home less than an hour, but she'd promised Willow they would make brownies as soon as she'd gotten off the bus. Now the baked treats were in the oven and dinner wasn't even started. Priorities—they had them in order. Lately, due to all the stress, Marly was either cleaning or baking. One was by far better for her waistline, but not nearly as comforting.

Marly glanced out the picture window in the living room and couldn't help but smile when she saw Drake's truck at the curb. No matter what she said to him about backing off, deep inside she was glad he hadn't.

Since when did she turn into a woman who played games? She didn't want to be that woman. Damn it, she was all on board with the friendship thing, but then he'd gone and kissed her, making her forget everything but the fact she wanted him on a more intimate level.

But she wouldn't risk the inevitable action Kevin would take if Marly moved on with another man.

The thought had her shivering as she flipped the lock and pulled the door open.

"Hey." Drake smiled, but the gesture didn't quite meet his eyes. "Can I come in?"

Stepping aside, Marly motioned for him to enter. Before she could question what was wrong, Willow came riding through the house on a hobby horse, donned in her cowgirl boots and a Native American headdress made out of construction paper.

"Hey, Chief! Did you come for a brownie?"

Drake squatted down and held up a small red fireman's helmet that he'd had hidden behind his back. "I actually came to give this to you."

Marly's heart melted…as if there was much more to melt where this man was concerned.

The horse dropped to the wood floor with a clatter as Willow jerked off her homemade headdress and threw it to the floor, promptly putting on her new helmet. "This is awesome! Thanks, Chief."

Drake patted the top of her hat. "You look like a natural."

Willow peered up from beneath the brim. "Does this mean you're here to give me a ride on the engine, too?"

Coming to his feet, Drake sighed. "Sorry, sweetheart, not today. But, if you can give me and your mom five minutes to talk, I have another surprise for you."

Willow squealed and clapped. "I'll give you six minutes. Because six is bigger than five."

Willow bounced back down the hall toward her bedroom, counting in a singsong voice without a care in the world. But as Marly turned her attention to Drake, she knew this man with the worry lines between his brows had something weighing heavily on his mind.

Without a word, Drake walked over to her couch and eased down, resting his elbows on his knees and his head in his hands. He didn't look at her, didn't say a word.

"Now you're really worrying me," she told him. "You haven't even flirted or tried to steal a kiss."

The joke was meant to get a reaction, but…nothing. Then another level of fear rose to the surface.

"Did you hear something about Jeremy?" she asked, crossing to sit in the secondhand accent chair adjacent to him. "Talk to me."

"It's not Jeremy." Raking his hands through his cropped hair, Drake let out a sigh and finally turned those worried blue eyes on her. "I'm sorry I just showed up like this."

"It's okay," she told him. "What happened?"

"I was suspended without pay until further notice."

"What?" Marly sat up straighter in her seat.

"The mayor insisted we let go of one more firefighter and I disagreed and informed him I refused to lay off any more of my men… I may have said a few other choice words, as well. In the end he figured I was the best candidate."

Marly hadn't seen Drake's temper. Well, she had, but only when he'd learned the ugly truth behind her scars. She honestly couldn't believe this was a man who would get violent.

"How does he expect my guys to keep working endless hours, doubling up on shifts and putting themselves in the line of danger every day when they're running on empty?"

Marly jerked back and stared at him. He was worried about his men? He wasn't worried about the fact that he would have no income?

"I can't wait until the election in a few months," Drake added.

A chill crept over Marly. The election. The reason for Kevin's threats...or one of the reasons. He wasn't lying when he said he'd find her. And when he did come looking, she had no clue how she could fight him. Because he would come. And the longer he waited before he lost patience, thinking she'd return, the angrier he'd be when he finally found her.

Marly shifted toward Drake. "Did you get that helmet for Willow before you talked to the mayor?"

Shaking his head, Drake eased back on her sofa and stretched his legs out in front of him. "No. I went back to the department and broke the news to the guys. I grabbed some things from my locker and the helmet for Willow."

Tears pricked her eyes. "That may be the sweetest thing anybody has ever done for her."

Drake shrugged and glanced away. "It's no big deal."

Obviously he wasn't a fan of her praise, but what man would get suspended and immediately think of the men he was leaving behind and a five-year-old little girl?

A hero. The title fit him perfectly, whether he wanted to wear it or not.

"Are the adults done talking?" Willow yelled from her bedroom.

Marly laughed. "You can come on out, honey."

"Good." Willow ran down the hallway. "I smell the brownies. Can I have one when they come out of the oven?"

"I don't think so, sweetie. After dinner, though."

Drake came to his feet. "I'll go. I don't want to disrupt your dinner."

"You said you had another surprise for me." Willow came to stand beside Drake, her helmet still resting atop her head and blond curls hanging down her back.

"Willow," Marly scolded in a half whisper. "If Drake needs to go, you just be thankful he brought you the helmet."

"I don't need to go," he retorted with a smile. "I just don't want to be in the way."

"You're not in the way." Willow grabbed his hand. "You wanna stay for supper?"

Marly couldn't ignore that tug on her heart at the sight of Willow's hand in Drake's. She was so trusting, so innocent. In some ways that was a blessing, because Willow had no idea why they were away from Kevin.

"I'm throwing some chicken on the grill," Marly told

him. "You're more than welcome to stay. As you've heard, we have brownies for dessert."

Drake's smile spread across his face as he looked from Marly to Willow and back to Marly. "It's the best offer I've had all day. Let me run out to the truck and get the other surprise."

Chapter Eleven

"That's good, but hold the ball like this."

Drake squatted down and turned the football until the laces were out. Covering Willow's delicate hand with his own, he drew her arm back and helped her launch it across the yard. Well, maybe not all the way across, but far enough to get a whoop of delight out of her.

"You did it." Drake gave her a high five and watched as she ran after the ball. "Come on, we'll do it again."

After assisting her about three more times, he let her go on her own. Each time she launched it in the air, she was jumping up and down.

"Here," he told her. "Let me stand down here and we'll pass it back and forth now that you've become a pro on me."

Willow laughed. "You'd better back up. I throw it far now."

To boost her newly found self-esteem, Drake backed up, knowing he could move forward pretty quickly to catch it.

"Dinner is ready," Marly called from the small patio area.

"Mama," Willow whined. "We were just starting to pass."

"You can pass later."

Leaving no room for discussion, Marly took a plate of chicken into the house and left the back door open, an invitation for them to follow.

Teaching this sweet little girl to play football—while wearing her cowgirl boots, no less—and going in to sit down to a home-cooked meal with a family felt very... right.

Growing up, his mother had always stressed the importance of family dinners, and he'd always known he would want that same connection, that same ritual with his own family.

He couldn't help but feel that tug right now, but he knew to keep his heart on guard. No matter what he might be ready for or might be feeling, Marly was still running scared.

Honestly, he was scared, too, but he was ready... or at least he was ready to try for more. The time had come for him to move forward, and he knew in his heart that Marly was the woman to move on with. Now if he could only get her to trust him... He had to give this a shot; he couldn't let this second chance go when it was right within reach.

Willow was standing on a stool washing her hands at the kitchen sink, and Drake went over to help Marly get plates ready.

"I'll take care of everything." She waved a hand toward the table. "Go have a seat."

Ignoring her orders, he pulled cups from the cabinet and filled them with ice, then poured lemonade from the pitcher she had sitting on the counter.

All too soon they were all gathered around the table, eating and passing the food around, after Willow had said the blessing. Drake cut up Willow's chicken while she chatted about her school day and how everyone was excited for the upcoming festival.

"Oh, I've got those flyers in my truck." He cut another piece of chicken, so thankful he didn't have to head home and microwave a hot dog. "I picked them up earlier today, but with everything else, I forgot."

"When can I get that engine ride?" Willow asked, shoving more chicken into her mouth.

"Honey, I'm not sure—"

Drake held up a hand and cut Marly off. "I am taking some time off work, but if you wouldn't mind a buddy of mine giving you a ride, I can set that up one day after school."

Even though Drake was looking at Willow, he saw Marly's eyes go wide. "Drake," she scolded.

"Tomorrow?" Willow asked, wide-eyed.

"As long as he's not out on a call," Drake promised with a smile. He loved seeing that hope in Willow's eyes, loved seeing how excited she got when discussing his own passion. "I'll let your mom know tomorrow."

They finished dinner, and Drake insisted on helping with the dishes. After a bit more passing the football with Willow, he hadn't realized how late it had gotten until Marly yelled out the back door that it was Willow's bath time. Drake picked up the ball, and by the time he'd gotten back in the house, Willow was nowhere to be seen. He heard water running in the bathroom down the hall and he assumed Marly was back there doing her nightly ritual. Alone.

He admired her. Not once had she complained or even acted as exhausted as he knew she had to be. Being a single mother working a full-time job had to be trying…not to mention dealing with whatever weighed heavily on her heart that she kept bottled inside. Independent and strong, she chose to face her battles head-on. She was a warrior.

Drake pulled his keys from his pocket and set the football on the end table. He wanted Willow to keep it. Who knows? Maybe he'd be back to pass with her again.

Just as he opened the front door, Marly called his name. When he glanced over his shoulder, she was holding a towel and washcloth.

"Don't leave," she said. "Can you give me twenty minutes to get her into bed?"

He'd give her all the time she wanted because the fact she wanted him to stay was a huge step.

"Sure." Drake nodded, pretending as though this wasn't an important milestone.

He barely caught a glimpse of her sweet smile as she

disappeared back down the hall. Drake took a seat on the couch and realized that since he'd been at Marly's, he hadn't thought of the mayor or his absurd suspension.

Wait until Cameron and Eli heard about this. They'd explode. They'd head down to the city council offices and stage a two-man protest.

Of course, Cameron was still working the undercover thing, so who knew when Drake would hear from him to even tell him about the issue.

When his cell chimed in his pocket, he pulled it out, but nothing showed up. Then he saw Marly's phone on the side table, near his arm. The face was lit up and he honestly wasn't trying to be nosy, but the glaring message was hard to miss.

You have 3 days left. I'm coming for you.

Above the cryptic message was *Kevin*. Must be the ex. Even his name sounded like a jerk.

Drake resisted the urge to pick up her phone and send this Kevin guy a message, but he wouldn't do anything to hurt Marly.

He didn't have to wait too long before Marly came back down the hall. The bottom of her gray T-shirt was damp, her hair was falling from her ponytail, and even though she looked like she could drop to sleep at any moment, to Drake, she looked beautiful.

"I don't know what you did to her, but she was out before I could finish cleaning up the bathroom."

Marly dropped to the sofa beside him, tipped her head back against the cushion and sighed.

The column of her throat was exposed, nearly begging to be kissed. But that she'd invited him to stay didn't mean she had something more in mind than just talking. Marly had the lead here and he would just have to follow…no matter how difficult holding himself back would be.

"Thank you." Turning her head against the cushion so she could face him, Marly offered a sweet, tired smile. "For the helmet, the football…for coming here and talking to me. After the way I left things at Eli's house, I was worried that maybe you wouldn't want to see me again."

Drake shifted, pulling his knee up onto the sofa. "You left because you were concerned about me. I'd be a jerk if I decided you weren't worth the trouble of seeing again. Besides, I wanted to give Willow the helmet and the football. Seeing you again is just icing on the proverbial cake."

Marly started to adjust her bangs, but Drake intercepted her hand and pulled it into his lap. "You look fine. Whether your scar is exposed or not, Marly. It doesn't define you."

Those brown doe eyes studied his face. Drake wanted to know what she saw, what she thought when she looked at him. He prayed she saw a man who truly cared for her, a man who would go as slow as she needed if she would just give him a sign that she would eventually be ready to trust and open up.

"What will you do about the suspension?" she asked, obviously dodging the topic of herself.

Drake continued to hold on to her hand. "Fight it.

There's a council meeting next week, and I plan on being there. I also plan on writing up a letter stating what all the mayor has done since taking office—the layoffs, the budget cuts, the new lights and flowers all around town that could've been one of my men back on the job. They can't expect the town to remain safe and out of debt as long as he's at the helm."

Marly turned her hand over in his so they were palm to palm. "You're pretty amazing. It's a rare man who would be more concerned about an entire town than his own suspension. I can't get over how you still thought of Willow during all of that."

Drake laced their fingers together. "It's not hard to think of people I care about, no matter what's going on in my life."

He didn't want to bring the ex into the picture, but he did want to get her reaction and see if perhaps this could lead to that open door he'd been waiting for.

"Your cell went off while you were back there," he told her. "A text from Kevin."

Her eyes widened for a second, then closed as she nodded. "I'm sure you saw what it said."

"I did."

Lifting her lids, she met his gaze. "And?"

"You have three more days," Drake told her. "Has he been threatening you still?"

Marly nodded. "He never stopped. I blackmailed him into giving me a divorce, but he's still under the impression I'll come back home."

"How did you blackmail him?"

Marly's free hand toyed with the ratty hem of her

T-shirt. "I have pictures," she told him. "Of me. I took them to the police."

Drake squeezed her hand, wanting her to continue, but at the same time he feared what she was about to reveal.

"He has friends on the force," she went on, still looking down at her damp shirt. "They have put me off for months, saying they would look into my allegations, but each time I call, I get the runaround again."

"Do they have these pictures?"

Marly nodded. "I also have copies."

"So what else did you threaten him with?" Drake asked.

With a sigh, Marly met his gaze. "I don't want to get into that. The bottom line is I left after he hurt me."

Drake's heart literally clenched at her bold confession. "He hurt you more than once."

He didn't ask; he knew. But her nod just confirmed his fear.

"Mentally at first," she murmured. "He controlled me, wanted me to be the perfect show wife. I mean, I have the blond hair and the curvy build, why would I want to work and use my degree when I could be arm candy and entice voters? He was appalled that I wanted to continue my work in the burn unit at the hospital."

Drake stroked the back of her hand with his thumb. "You're an amazing nurse, Marly."

"I love what I do," she stated. "But when I got pregnant with Willow, he demanded I stop. That's when he started getting violent."

Drake wanted to rip this guy's head off. What lowlife hit a woman, let alone a pregnant one? There was no excuse for his behavior. Absolutely none.

"I don't want to get into the details," she added. "I've made a break, I'm trying to start fresh and give Willow a better life. She didn't witness any abuse—actually, her father ignored her most of her life. He didn't want to be bothered with annoyances such as teething, potty training, random sicknesses. He also wasn't thrilled that her personality tended to stray toward tomboy and not a meek, quiet little girl."

"The more I hear, the more I hate this man." Drake tried to keep his tone level, but he was seriously starting to feel his blood pressure soar. "I know I'm not Willow's father, but I just don't see how anybody could look at her and not fall in love. She's an amazing little girl, so full of life."

Marly's sad face softened with a genuine smile. "She's everything to me. I'm not sure I would've had the courage to leave if not for her. I just knew I never wanted her to see that, never wanted her to think abuse of any kind was okay. I want her to grow up and fall in love and not worry about saying or doing something wrong."

Drake couldn't stop himself from reaching with his free hand to stroke the side of her face. "And what about you? Do you want to fall in love and not worry?"

Marly closed her eyes, turning her face just slightly toward his hand. Drake cupped her cheek, stroking the dark circle beneath her eye. He hated how hard she worked, how much she pushed herself.

"I'd love to fall in love," she whispered. "I had a fantasy as a little girl that I would marry the man of my dreams. No little girl ever dreams of being neglected, taken for granted…abused. But I'm getting stronger every single day. I won't let myself get that low again. Ever."

She whispered the word *abused* as if it were a disease. In a sense, Drake figured it was. The word alone crippled her, made her feel inferior and less than who she was, which was a vibrant woman, beautiful and courageous.

"I won't let him get to you, Marly. You're safe here."

Her eyes searched his. "Nobody can stop him."

"I guarantee I'm more determined to keep you safe than he is to get you back." Drake would lay down his life for Marly and Willow. The raw emotions threatened to have him taking charge of her situation, but he knew she needed to remain in control. "Trust me."

Marly's hand came up to his face, the stubble on his jaw bristling beneath her palm. He loved those soft hands on him, loved how she was slowly reaching out to him, literally and figuratively. Little by little he was breaking her barriers of defense down, and he'd scale over anything that was left.

"I trust you," she told him with a smile. "You lost your job and immediately thought of everyone else around you. You're a good man."

Drake laughed. "I should've gotten suspended weeks ago. I had no idea that was what it would take to win your trust."

"I didn't expect to trust again, especially so fast." Marly dropped her hand and settled it over their entwined fingers still in his lap. "You do something to me, Drake. At first I was afraid of how fast my emotions were spiraling toward you. I mean, how could I trust anything I felt after what I'd lived through? But you're a different man than he was and I'm still getting used to the fact that you know how to treat a woman, and you know when to be patient."

"My patience skills are really being tested right now," he told her with a smile. "Because all I want to do is kiss you."

Drake was utterly shocked when Marly scooted in, held on to his hand and slid her mouth over his. As he opened to her he felt as if he'd won some sort of lottery. She was kissing him. She'd never initiated anything before, and here she was taking charge.

With his free hand, Drake cupped his hand around the nape of her neck and changed the angle of the kiss so he could get better access. With his knee between them, it was hard to get the closeness he craved, so he adjusted his body, putting his feet on the floor, and inched closer to Marly.

Her hands slid from his and traveled up over his T-shirt. She gripped his shoulders as she moved closer, as well. Her passion was evident, and Drake wanted more…as much as she was willing to give.

Drake broke free of her sensual lips and kissed his way down her neck. Marly arched her back, still holding on to his shoulders. He still needed more.

Snaking his hands up under her oversize shirt, Drake nearly whimpered when his fingertips came in contact with smooth skin. He traveled on up until his thumbs brushed the underside of her satin bra. He pulled her cups down with both hands and filled his palms with her softness. Marly let out a low moan that shot straight to his gut and had him lifting her shirt.

"You're stunning," he told her, ducking his head to taste her.

Marly cupped the side of his head as if holding him in position. With her back arched, Drake eased her down until she lay on the sofa. He brought himself over her, never breaking contact.

When her hands went back to his shoulders, it took him a moment to realize she wasn't clenching anymore but pushing. He lifted his head, glanced down at her face to see that she'd gone pale.

"I'm sorry," she whispered. "This is… I can't…"

He lifted himself off her, wondering what part had scared her.

"Don't apologize," he told her, reaching down to adjust her shirt. "I shouldn't have pushed."

With shaky hands, she smoothed her shirt herself and sat up…on the other end of the sofa. "No, no. You didn't do anything I didn't want. I just wasn't expecting to be so nervous. But when I felt your weight on me…"

Her voice cracked as she put her hand over her mouth and shook her head. The unspoken words slammed into Drake and he knew… Damn it, he knew full well what she'd endured at the hands of her ex.

Now more than ever he vowed she would not fall victim to that man again. He had to tamp down his fury, keep it hidden so as not to scare her further.

But he would be making a call to his police chief

brother to see what they could do, since he wouldn't allow Marly to live in fear any longer. Her superwoman act had to end because while he was perfectly aware she could stand on her own, he didn't want her to. He wanted to be the one she leaned on, the one she came to for support and when she was afraid.

"I'm not ready," she whispered, her voice thick with emotion. "I understand if that's not what you wanted to hear, if you want to move on."

When she turned to face him with tears in her eyes, Drake's heart broke for her.

"I mean, you're ready to move on, you've said that," she added. "Waiting on me would be like working backward."

Drake reached across the gap between them and held her face in his hands until she kept her watery doe eyes on him. "Waiting for you isn't working backward. Waiting on you is definitely a step in the right direction... for both of us. You need support, emotionally if nothing else, and I damn well will be the one to provide it. I won't do anything you aren't ready for, Marly, but I'm not walking away because you're vulnerable and you're afraid."

One lone tear slid down her cheek. "I wish I'd found you first."

Her bold, raw revelation pierced his heart. "You found me last. That's what matters."

Chapter Twelve

Drake slid another coat of mud on the drywall to hide the nails and the tape. Soon this room would be... something. He really didn't know what he'd do with the addition to the back of his house. He'd originally started this project as a way to vent after Andrea's death. She had died as a result of his driving, a detail from the accident that he liked to keep in the deepest, darkest recesses of his mind.

Using his hands, building something and actually having control over the outcome had been great therapy.

Now, however, the target of his rage was Kevin. The haunted, frightened look in Marly's eyes burned in his mind. Another man may have been the one to put that level of fear in her, but Drake would damn well be the man to take it out.

He hadn't been lying when he'd told her he was the last man to enter her life. He wanted to be that last man, and the revelation shocked the hell out of him...but in a good way.

Since Andrea's death, he'd been so cautious about whom he asked out, but everything about Marly seemed to click into place with his life and his desires. Definitely his desires.

On every level he wanted to make her happy, wanted to see a light in her eyes that he only saw when she spoke of her daughter.

And Willow? She'd totally stolen his heart from day one. How was she taking all of this? The move, being away from her father... Of course, if she was being ignored or brushed aside by her dad, perhaps she didn't even miss him.

The sweet girl had no idea the joy of that family bond. Drake had grown up with such a tight-knit family, between his affectionate parents and his hellion brothers. Of course they clashed at times—what family didn't?—but they were always there for each other, always supportive.

Drake swiped his wide spatula over the glop of mud and wiped the excess against the tray he held. He jerked his head around when he heard his front door open and shut. Heavy footsteps sounded down the hallway.

When his brother Cameron poked his head in, Drake went back to work.

"Grab that other tray and make yourself useful," Drake told him.

"Your warm greetings always make me want to stop and visit more often."

Cameron rattled around behind him and Drake smiled. He knew Cameron also chased demons away by doing physical labor. Of course, Cameron was private and nobody knew what was eating at him lately.

"It's looking good," Cameron commented. "Figure out what you're going to use this for?"

"Not a clue." Drake glanced over his shoulder and pointed with his spatula. "That bucket is the one I've been dipping out of."

"Heard you got suspended."

Drake cringed. "Yeah. Mayor Jerkwad decided that we needed another man in my department cut. When I refused to lay off another hard worker, he opted to remove me."

"This won't stick," Cameron assured him. "And he won't get reelected."

Drake nodded. "I know, but that man just lives to be a nuisance."

"Wanna talk about it?" Cameron asked.

"If I did, I'd go on some talk show and cry in front of the nation. I'm good."

They worked in silence for a few minutes. Obviously something was on Cameron's mind or he wouldn't have stopped by, but Drake knew his older brother well enough to know not to push.

"Hear you have a woman."

Drake laughed, dropping his spatula into the tray. "That's not what I thought you'd lead in with, but yeah, I guess I do."

"Heard she's a pretty nurse with a cute kid." Cameron turned, glancing over his shoulder. "You ready for all of that?"

Drake nodded. "I wasn't sure if I was at first, but I am now."

He moved on to the next wall and started covering up the nails. "While we're on the topic, I know you're swamped with whatever has had you away from us for months, but I need you to run a check on someone."

"Who?"

"Her ex."

"Come on, Drake. You can't be running a background check on an ex," Cameron complained with a snort.

Dropping his spatula into the mud, Drake turned and leaned against the dry part of the wall. "He's abusive, Cameron."

His brother turned as well and cursed beneath his breath. "All right. Give me the details you have."

"From what Marly says, he's powerful. I don't know what she means by that. His first name is Kevin."

Cameron's brows raised. "And? That's all?"

"Her last name is Haskins. I assume that's his, as well." Something clicked in his mind. "Kevin Haskins," he whispered. "Oh, hell."

Cameron's brows shot up. "You're dating the ex-wife of the state representative?"

Powerful, wanting a perfect family image... Drake should've guessed he was a politician. His gut churned, and everything she'd ever told him made him sick to his stomach.

"Damn it." Drake took a seat on the lid of a bucket of mud and sat his tray next to him on the subfloor. "No wonder she's afraid for me."

"Excuse me?"

Drake eyed his brother. "She told me I couldn't get involved because her ex would ruin me and my career. I had no idea he was that powerful."

"Are you going to back down?" Cameron asked.

"What do you think?"

Cameron laughed. "I think Kevin has one hell of a fight on his hands. The man's a politician. I've no doubt he's got some skeletons hidden in his dirty closet."

Drake nodded. "I don't care what you find, how minor it is, let me know. She's got pictures of the abuse."

"Why hasn't she taken them to the cops?" Cameron asked, finding the lid to the used bucket and putting it on so he could take a seat. "She could get a restraining order."

"She did take them," Drake corrected. "She was told they'd look into it and that was months ago. They keep giving her the runaround, and she figures Kevin has the Nashville PD in his pocket."

Cameron swore again, and the muscles in his tattooed forearm flexed as he tightened his grip on the tray in his hand. "I'll look into it myself. I'm busy, but not too busy to bury a dirty, wife-beating politician. The little girl... Did he ever—"

"No." Drake shook his head. "Marly said he basically ignored her."

"Well, that's something. I've got a good friend who's an investigator. He'll make this top priority."

"Let me know what I owe him."

Cameron nodded. "He works cheap for me, but I'll let you know."

"So what brought you here?" Drake asked. "Because I know it wasn't to spackle—as glamorous as this job is."

Cameron sighed. "I've just got a lot going on and needed a break. Figured you'd be here working."

"You want a beer?" Drake offered.

"Nah. I've got to be somewhere this evening and I need to be alert. Although having a couple of beers doesn't sound bad right now."

Drake came to his feet, stretching out the kink in his back from installing the new drywall on the ceiling last night after he'd left Marly's house.

"How soon will you be wrapping up this mysterious case?" Drake asked, picking up his tray to get back to work.

"I have no idea. Soon, I hope, but realistically, probably not for at least another month."

"Is something big going on in town, or are you working with another department?"

Behind him, he heard Cameron getting back to work, as well. "I can't say much, but it's my department and other law enforcement. If everything goes down as it should, this will be epic."

Drake knew Cameron's job was dangerous, hell, his own was dangerous, but he couldn't help but worry about his brother's state of mind. Going deep under-cover wasn't something the chief did often, but Drake knew his brother wasn't about to sit on the sidelines and let other people go after the bad guys.

"Is there something in particular about this case that's bothering you, or is it just the overall red tape and jumping through hoops to make sure the suspect is brought down right?"

Cameron let out a faint laugh. "Oh, the jumping through hoops is always the bane of my existence, but there's more with this case."

Drake wasn't stupid, and knew his brother well enough to read between the lines. "A woman?" he asked.

"Possibly."

"She the perp?" Drake asked.

"No, but she may be getting caught in the middle."

No wonder Cameron needed to vent and blow off some steam. But there were other ways to do it besides putting up drywall. His brother was as much of a protector as Drake and Eli were.

"How about a game of one-on-one?" Drake suggested.

Cameron shrugged. "I suppose I could kick your butt before I head in."

"Please. You're an old man, exhausted from staying out too late. I'll win this match in no time and you'll still have time for a nap before you go to work."

Cameron flipped him the finger. Drake hated what his brother was going through, hated that he was torn between his emotions and loyalty to his work.

But Cameron was a strong man and an even stronger cop, and Drake had every confidence in the world that Cameron would find dirt on Kevin. Because even though Marly was afraid for him, he wasn't afraid one bit.

Angry, yes; ready to fight all of her battles, definitely, but not afraid.

Regardless, in the end, Drake would get what he wanted. And he wanted Marly and Willow in his life.

Chapter Thirteen

Willow had finally gotten her engine ride thanks to Drake's second-in-command, Tyler Warren. Tyler was a sucker for kids and Willow was one easy child to fall for…especially when she'd shown up in her worn cowgirl boots and the fireman's helmet Drake had given her.

Not only had Willow ridden in the engine, Drake and Marly had gone along for the ride, too. He wondered if the mayor saw him riding around in the engine. Honestly, he didn't care. He wasn't breaking any rules—he wasn't driving, he wasn't in any type of uniform and he hadn't even worn one of his SFD tees.

Regardless if the mayor saw them or not, Drake would still put Willow's wishes and his promise to her ahead of Tipton and his moronic rules.

"How about I take her on a tour of the station?" the

assistant chief asked. "I'm sure she'd love the behind-the-scenes tour we didn't give her class."

Drake looked at Marly. "I don't care," she told them. "I just don't want her to be in your way."

Tyler shook his head. "Impossible for her to be in my way."

Willow jumped up and down, holding on to her fireman's helmet with her hands. "This is the best day ever," she squealed.

Willow grabbed Tyler's hand and practically pulled him into the department's open bay. Drake laughed and turned to face Marly.

"He's a sucker for kids. He'll do anything she wants. Don't be surprised if she comes home with a T-shirt."

Marly smiled. "I'm just thrilled she's so happy. I worried about moving her out of Nashville, but she has really taken to the small-town life."

"Have you taken to the small-town life?" he asked, taking her hand and pulling her toward the back of the department, where there was a bench in the shade...and away from the street with nosy onlookers.

They took a seat, and Drake didn't even try to sit away from her. He wanted her to get used to the feel of him beside her. He wanted her to not worry about anything but the way they were so obviously meant to be on this path of healing together.

"I can't believe the festival is in just a few days," she told him, turning her face up to the soft breeze.

"I'll be glad when we can present a check to Shawn and Amy. They have to be running on fumes going back and forth, taking turns being with Jeremy and trying to keep their business up and running here."

Marly nodded. "I know. Good news, though. I called to check on Jeremy earlier today, and his first surgery went even better than the doctors had expected. He's doing really well."

Relief swept through Drake. "That's great, Marly."

Drake wrapped an arm around her and rested his hand on her shoulder. That was something else he wanted her to get used to—his random touch. Being near her and not seeking that contact was nearly impossible, but she needed to discover the positive aspect of touches from a man. She needed to know what a normal, caring relationship was about, and if he had to take baby steps to get her to that point, then so be it.

She stiffened just for a second, then relaxed against his side. "You're going to spoil me."

Drake grinned. "That's the plan."

She leveled him with her sweet smile, her eyes seeking his. "What else is in your plan?"

"To stop Kevin Haskins from getting near you or Willow."

Marly gasped, her eyes widened and she went pale. Damn it, he hadn't meant to blurt that out, but he wasn't thinking straight.

"Drake," she whispered. "Please, you can't."

Now that she knew that he was perfectly aware of who she was running scared from, Drake decided to lay it all on the line. She needed to know someone was fighting for her, needed to know that someone was him and that he wasn't giving up just because things may be getting a bit difficult.

"I can and I will," he insisted. "Kevin may be powerful, but I guarantee I've got more motivation and drive. Guys like him just pay people off, thinking that will get them ahead. You're living in Stonerock now, and he has no one on this police force in his pocket."

The determination in Drake's tone sent shivers through Marly despite the early-fall temperatures.

"You have no idea what you're up against." A tremble rippled through her at the endless, terrifying possibilities. "Have you involved your brother?"

Drake merely stared at her, not answering her question.

"You can't do this," she all but cried. "First of all, he will not only ruin your career, he will ruin Cameron's if he's gotten involved. Not to mention this will give him ammunition to take Willow. You can't just steamroll me and think you can decide what is best without talking to me."

"I talked to you, Marly. I've told you over and over that I wouldn't let anyone hurt you or Willow." Drake pushed forward off the back of the bench until he was leaning in toward her. "Just because I know who your ex is now changes nothing from my standpoint. I will still protect you, I will still keep you safe and I will still keep trying to get you to see that I'm not going anywhere."

Marly battled the urge to throw her arms around his neck and revel in the strength and protection he so freely offered.

Coming to her feet, Marly brushed her hair behind her shoulders. "I can't live through this. I can't be with someone who would go behind my back and try to control my future."

"And were you planning on being with me?" he asked, slowly rising to his feet. "Were you planning on fully taking that guard down and letting me in?"

Was she? She was certainly headed in that direction.

Marly smoothed her hand over her bangs and shook her head. "I don't know, Drake. I just know this is a mistake. Going beyond friendship is impossible."

Drake rested his hands on his hips, his eyes never leaving hers. "Fine."

Taken aback by his simple reaction, Marly crossed her arms over her chest. "Fine? That's all you have to say?"

Drake shrugged. "I can still care about you and respect your wishes. If friendship is all you can give, I'll take it. But I won't stop caring, so you can't ask me to."

The man was relentless. He knew what he wanted, had this notion that they could help each other. And he might be right, but...could she take that chance? Could she risk his life by pulling him into her nightmare?

"Let's take Willow for some ice cream."

Marly laughed. "What?"

"Things have been too intense with us lately," he told her with that grin that never failed to melt her. "We need to relax, just have fun. Friends go for ice cream, don't they?"

How could she argue with that logic?

"If Willow found out I turned down ice cream, she would never forgive me."

Drake held out his hand. "Then let's go get her. We'll pick up the ice cream and go sit in the park. There's a bridge there where you can throw bread crumbs and feed the ducks."

Marly looked from his outstretched hand to his eyes. "And you have bread crumbs on you?"

"No, smarty pants." He reached down and grabbed her hand when she didn't take his invitation. "We'll swing by the store and get a loaf. Have you taken Willow to the park yet?"

"We went there for a walk a few times, but we haven't fed the ducks. She'll love it."

Drake led her toward the front of the department, but stopped short of the open bay. When he tugged on her hand to turn her to face him, Marly put her other hand on his chest to prevent falling.

He tipped her head up and captured her lips in a brief, yet potent, powerful kiss. Barely lifting his head, he stroked her bottom lip, which was still tingling from the all-too-short encounter.

"You may be stuck in this friendship phase, but you should know, I've moved past that." He nipped at her lips once more. "When you're ready to catch up with me, let me know."

With that, he left her standing in the sunshine, wondering what in the world she was going to do with all of her emotions, her wants and desires.

How could they remain just friends when she'd had a taste of that sensual mouth, knew how arousing his touch could be, had experienced that selfless generosity he so freely gave?

Willow's sweet squeal sounded from inside the department. Marly smiled. Had her father ever gotten that reaction from her? Had her own father ever surprised her with anything so simple as ice cream and a trip to a park?

Something stirred deep within Marly. No matter what she told Drake, what barriers she tried to put between them, he'd managed to break through each wall. He'd managed to penetrate her heart.

God help her… She was falling in love with him.

The morning of the festival was already promising a beautiful sunny day. Marly stuck signs on each table, stating what each station was: face painting, pie tossing, bake sale, silent auction.

She'd had days to think about her growing feelings for Drake and she was still a mess. He'd not made another move, hadn't kissed her again and had been totally, 100 percent…friendly.

Darn that man.

Of course, she was giving mixed signals because her heart and her mind were battling for dominance. And her heart was winning.

Glancing around, she spotted Drake and his brother Eli speaking to an elderly woman. Marly smiled. The two strong men towered over the lady holding a rhinestone cane and wearing a hot pink skirt and…heels?

Marly laughed and turned just as a middle-aged woman came up to the table.

"You must be Marly."

Nodding, Marly smiled. "I am."

"I'm Drake's mother. You can call me Bev." Her eyes darted to the distance and back. "Bless her heart. Maddie Mays always bakes the most unusual breads and gives them as gifts. I suppose she's donating to the bake sale."

Intrigued, Marly tilted her head. "Unusual breads?"

Bev laughed. "Pomegranate pumpkin, kale and strawberries... Never just a traditional banana or zucchini."

Marly made a mental note to bypass those "specialty" breads.

"But she was my husband's best patient, and now she has a soft spot for Eli. Of course, she randomly injures herself pole dancing."

Marly froze, her eyes wide. "I'm sorry. Did you say..."

"Pole dancing," Bev confirmed. "She has a pole in her living room and that's how she says she gets her workout in."

Marly couldn't help the bubble of laughter that escaped. "Well, here I just walk or jog for exercise. Apparently I'm boring."

"According to everyone I've spoken to, you're far from boring," Drake's mom said with a soft smile. "I've heard you described as quiet, sweet, caring, a great nurse and wonderful mother. Sounds like quite a full plate of excitement to me."

Marly didn't say anything... What could she say? Drake's mother asking about her was exactly what

Marly would do as a mother. She couldn't blame the woman.

"Oh, I'm sorry," Bev said, patting Marly's arm. "I didn't mean to make you feel awkward. If it helps, I'm a little out of my element, too. I mean, it's been so long since Drake allowed any woman to occupy his time. I'm just so thankful he met you, and I had to see you for myself."

Marly smiled. "I understand. I have a little girl, so I get the curious-mom feeling."

Bev's smile was so warm, so caring. Marly knew this woman had her hands full with three boys, yet she still seemed…soft, sweet.

"Well, two amazing ladies standing by the silent auction table." Drake came up to stand next to his mother, giving her a kiss on the cheek. "People will pull out the checkbooks for you two, for sure."

Drake's mom smacked him in the stomach. "You hush. Nobody could afford us. Isn't that right, darling?"

Marly nodded. "Afraid so. Especially because I come with an adorable little tomboy."

"Oh, where is she?" Bev clapped her hands together. "I've heard just how wonderful she is and I can't wait to meet her."

Marly smiled, glancing over to where Willow sat beneath a large oak tree, petting a giant mixed-breed dog, which was just one of the many Eli's wife, Nora, had brought for kids to play with from the local no-kill animal shelter.

"That's her," Marly said, pointing. "I may never get her away from those dogs."

"She's an animal lover, huh?" Bev asked. "What kind of dog does she have?"

Marly swallowed. "Um…we don't have a dog. We just moved here and…"

"Mom, can you go help Eli?" Drake chimed in. "He was setting up the bake sale area and I have a feeling he'll be sampling the goods if you don't keep an eye on him."

Bev patted his cheek, as if Drake were still her little boy. "I know when you're trying to get rid of me, but you're right. With Nora busy, Eli will eat everything in sight if left alone." She turned and smiled at Marly. "It was a pleasure to meet you. Have Drake bring you by for dinner so we can talk more."

"I'd like that," Marly told her, realizing just how true the statement was.

Once she was gone, Drake turned to Marly. "Sorry about that. I should've warned you my mother would be here."

Shrugging, Marly shoved her hair behind her ears. "It's no problem at all. She's great."

"Yeah, she is, but I'm sorry about the dog comment. She has no clue about your history. She only knows who you are right here."

"Too bad I'm not that person for real," she muttered.

"You are that person, Marly," he told her, resting his hands on her shoulders. "You're the caring nurse, the festival coordinator, loving mother. You're out from under Kevin's thumb, so anything you're doing now is the real Marly and who you want to be."

He was right. This was her. The small-town life,

the laid-back atmosphere, the community where people came together to help when one of their own was hurting. This was what she'd yearned for while being a picture-perfect wife for so long.

Willow's laughter cut through the park, and Marly glanced over to see her getting her face licked by an adorable little puppy.

"I need to get her a dog," Marly murmured. "She's never asked. How could I not see this?"

Drake squeezed her shoulders until she faced him once again. "You were a little busy setting up a stable life and keeping you and your daughter protected."

"I know, but I still can't ignore the fact she's a child and it's my job to create memories for her."

Drake ducked his head just a tad until his bright blue eyes met hers. The smile he offered had her heart doing flips.

"You chose the rental house with a tree house, you're letting her help with this festival, we gave her a ride on a fire engine… I'd say she's already formed some pretty great memories since you've moved here."

Reaching up to hold on to his thick wrists, Marly tilted her head. "You're right. Parenting is hard. I just want to give her everything."

"You're doing an amazing job."

Marly glanced to the side and noticed a few older ladies staring in their direction. The women had purses on their wrists, pearls around their necks and smiles on their faces.

"We're being watched," Marly whispered.

Drake laughed. "Small-town life. Your business is everyone's business."

Groaning, Marly closed her eyes. "They think we're...we're..."

"Lovers?" he whispered next to her ear, his warm breath tickling the side of her neck.

Her eyes flew open; she dropped her hands from his wrists. "We are friends. That's it."

Drake's smirk had Marly backing up. "For now," he told her.

Squinting her eyes at him, Marly held up a finger. "Don't put words in my mouth. You know where I stand on this."

Laughing, Drake inched closer with each step back she took. "Oh, I know what you said, but I also know what you're not saying."

Holding up both hands, Marly gritted her teeth. "Stop. Right there. I've got things to do and you're distracting me."

"That's part of my evil ploy."

She turned, but stopped when he whispered, "If you stomp off, they'll think we had a lovers' spat."

Clenching her fists, Marly did the only thing she could think to do. She turned around and kissed him. Full on the mouth, hands gripping his shoulders.

Then she pulled away and gave him a shove.

"There," she told him. "Now they'll be all confused and ask you about the girl you're seeing. What will you tell them about us?"

His eyes widened; his nostrils flared. Desire settled into his eyes, and Marly turned and walked away before she did something really crazy…like drag him back to her house. Because lately, more and more, she wanted to do just that.

And now she had to figure out what she wanted. Did she want to live in fear or did she want to finally go after something that would make her happy, something that would make her future—and that of her precious daughter—brighter?

Chapter Fourteen

"Looks like a great turnout, Chief."

Drake cringed inwardly at the voice that was literally mocking him. He'd come over to the face-painting table to see Willow get transformed into a puppy, but now he'd have to turn and confront the one person he wished he could go the rest of his life without seeing.

On a sigh, Drake opted to be the bigger man here as he pushed away from the table and turned.

"That's what we were hoping for," Drake told him. "What are you into? Getting your face painted?"

Oh, the endless jokes Drake could come up with about options for the paint job. But for now he would play it like the upstanding, albeit suspended, citizen he was.

"Just came out to support the family in need," the mayor stated, his tone higher no doubt so people could hear.

Drake didn't miss the fact that the smarmy guy didn't even know Shawn and Amy's names. This little publicity stunt made Drake loathe the man even more.

Drake also highly doubted the jerk would take out his wallet to make a contribution of any kind. Oh, if the newspaper were around, he might.

"I trust you'll be at the council meeting on Monday?"

Drake gritted his teeth and forced himself to remain calm. "Wouldn't miss it."

Mayor Tipton leaned in and lowered his tone. "Just try to control yourself there, Chief. We wouldn't want you to get permanently removed from your position."

Drake reached behind him, absently reaching for a brush sitting in a cup of paint. His fingertips slid carefully along the table until he found one. Bingo. He swirled it around to get it good and coated.

"Oh, I can control myself," Drake stated with a smile. "Oh, here comes Carrie from the *Daily Times*. You'll want to make sure you get a good picture so she can write up all the lies you pay her to print."

His face reddened. "You better watch it. You're skating on thin ice."

Carrie approached. "Mayor, could I get a picture of you with the chief?"

Oh, the timing... Drake couldn't have planned it better himself. Just as she raised the camera, Drake pulled the brush from the cup and streaked it across Tipton's nose. And glory, glory—without even looking, Drake had been dipping the brush in hot pink.

"You…" The mayor stumbled over his words and Drake thought his head was going to explode. "How dare you."

Drake turned, placed the brush back into the cup and gave a wide-eyed Willow a wink. "It's paint. It'll wash off. Although I'm sure one of these lovely high school students from the art program would love to finish my masterpiece. I don't have time right now. I have to go check on the dunking booth. I assume you'll be heading there next to wash off the paint?"

The mayor's jaw clenched, his eyes narrowed. "I'll see you Monday."

Drake held out his hand for Willow to take, and he pulled her to his side. "Can't wait."

The pies were gone, the bake sale table empty, and the silent auction had raked in more money than they could have ever dreamed of. Marly couldn't wait to present the check to Shawn and Amy. Neither had been able to make it today, understandably, but it seemed as though all of Stonerock had come to show their support for sweet Jeremy.

Even Mayor Tipton had made an appearance…and the highlight of the day was when Drake had "accidentally" painted the man's face. Marly had mentally high-fived Drake for the genius move, knowing full well he couldn't help himself. Actually, the mayor should be glad Drake had only settled for the immature act.

Marly knew Mayor Tipton's type. He'd only come for the grand show of it all. He needed to be seen, have a few pictures taken and offer fake smiles and empty promises.

Yeah, she knew his kind all too well. And Marly knew one thing for sure: if she was still here when election time came around, he certainly wasn't getting her vote.

Drake and Eli were loading tables onto the back of Drake's truck. Willow was with Drake's mother, and from the looks of it, those two had become fast friends. The love these virtual strangers had shown Marly's daughter was overwhelming. They had taken Marly and Willow in without question…all because of Drake.

Marly loaded all the signs and the cash box into her car. After locking the doors, she set out to find Willow. Of course, she was still with Drake's mother and the two were headed her way…hand in hand.

"Thank you so much for staying with her while we packed up," Marly told Bev as they approached.

"Oh, she was an absolute delight. I raised three boys, so having a girl around is quite different, but fun."

Willow bounced from one foot to another. "Mrs. St. John said I could come over and spend the night. She said we could watch movies and make cookies and then for breakfast she would make her famous French toast."

Marly jerked her gaze back to Bev. "Oh, um…"

"I was serious," Drake's mother said with a smile. "I'd love to have her over, but I completely understand if you don't want her to. I mean, you barely know me."

Marly swallowed, more than surprised that this woman would welcome Willow into her home so freely.

"Please, Mommy," Willow begged, still holding on

to Bev's hand. "I promise I'll be a big girl and I'll be good for Mrs. St. John."

Torn, Marly looked between the older woman and Willow. Both held the same hopeful look on their faces. Marly couldn't help but laugh.

"Are you sure?" Marly asked. "I don't want you to feel put on the spot."

"Oh, honey. I invited her, she didn't ask me." Bev looked down at Willow and winked. "Besides, I just discovered my new friend here loves *Mulan*, and that happens to be one of my favorite movies."

"Because she's so strong," Willow beamed. "She doesn't care about a crown or a dress. She's the coolest."

Marly shrugged. "How can I argue, then?"

"Why don't I go ahead and take her home?" Bev suggested. "Take your time cleaning up here and just run her pajamas by anytime."

Bev gave Marly the address, and Marly barely got a kiss before Willow skipped away with Drake's mother.

No, Marly would never let Willow go to the house of someone that Marly had just met, but she was confident that Bev wasn't some ogre or would put her child in danger. The woman had managed to raise three strong, upstanding men.

Once the park looked back in shape, the random garbage was picked up, all tables were loaded and Cameron and crew had headed back to the police station, Marly found herself alone with Drake.

"Where's Willow?" he asked, shoving his hands into his pockets.

"Believe it or not, she went for a sleepover with your mother."

Drake laughed. "Oh, I believe it. She's been chomping at the bit to get grandchildren. My brothers and I have tried to rein her back in, but she's so excited. Now that Eli has one, she's backed off me and Cameron."

Marly yawned. "Sorry," she muttered around her hand. "I'm exhausted, but this was a good day."

"Any idea how much we brought in yet?"

Marly shook her head. "I know we have at least a couple thousand, but I plan on counting it all later once I'm not so sleepy."

"Need me to follow you home?" he asked, his brows drawn together.

His genuine concern continued to win her over.

"No, I'm fine. I'll call you later tonight or tomorrow with the amount and we can go present Shawn and Amy with a check when we can catch one of them at their store."

"Sounds good to me."

He stared at her for another moment. The sun had started setting, and the air had turned a bit cooler now. But the shiver that raced through her had nothing to do with the dropping evening temperatures and everything to do with the man who stood before her and had made it no secret that he wanted more than friendship.

"If you need anything or if you run into a problem, don't try to be a hero. Call me." Drake slid her hair away from her face, pushing her bangs away where she knew he could see her scar. "I expect nothing in return. You know that, right?"

Marly nodded. "I'll call if I need you."

And those words held so much more meaning than she'd intended.

"See you later," she told him, needing to get home and get Willow's things gathered.

Drake nodded his goodbye, and a part of Marly was relieved he was letting her go without the flirting. But then she realized he was giving her the space she'd requested, he was being noble and, darn him, he was letting her decide what she really wanted.

Marly drove home and grabbed some pajamas, clothes for tomorrow, a toothbrush and Willow's favorite pillow. After shoving it all in Willow's small horse tote bag, she headed back out. She'd stashed the money box in her bedroom and intended to count the proceeds as soon as possible. Hanging on to that much cash made her nervous. Money was Kevin's thing... It had never been hers.

Turned out Drake's parents didn't live far from Marly at all. That was an added comfort. The neighborhood with its tree-lined streets and simple cottages with window boxes full of colorful flowers and neatly manicured lawns just screamed small-town USA. Marly wanted to be a part of this community more than she'd first thought possible.

In the beginning, coming to Stonerock had just been a means of escape. But now that she was here, Marly realized she wanted to stay, wanted to put down roots here for herself and her daughter.

After Marly dropped off the bag and got in one more kiss good-night from Willow, she was more than ready to go home, soak in a tub and do absolutely nothing. When was the last time she'd done nothing? Or pampered herself? She didn't have to work tomorrow and she planned on taking advantage of that fact.

She started her engine and pulled out of the subdivision, but instead of heading home, she turned toward Drake's house. She'd never been to his house, but he'd told her where he lived and she figured she'd just drive by to see it…just in case she ever wanted to visit.

Oh, who was she kidding?

Pulling into his drive behind his black truck, Marly called herself all kinds of fool for being there.

But for once in her life, she wasn't going to second-guess herself. So before she could sit in her used SUV and talk herself out of it, she jerked open the door and marched right up to his entrance. She knocked on the door and waited. Nerves were starting to consume her, but before she could turn and walk away, the door swung wide-open and Drake stood there wearing only a towel and water droplets all across his bare, chiseled chest.

Marly's eyes widened as she took her visual sampling of the man who had consumed her thoughts, her fantasies, for weeks.

"You flatter me with that look," he said with a grin. "But I'm assuming you didn't come here to stare at my chest."

Digging up courage from deep within, Marly squared her shoulders and placed a hand on his chest. The hair between his pecs tickled her palm.

"That's where you would be wrong," she told him,

backing him into his living room. "I did come here to stare at your chest, and to take you up on your offer of going beyond friends."

His heavy hand came up to cover hers. "Not that I'm complaining, but why the change of heart?"

Marly focused on his mouth, his eyes. "Because I'm finally taking what I want. And I want you."

Chapter Fifteen

Drake had waited for this moment. Had fantasized about it to the point where it had become real in his mind.

But nothing had prepared him for the confident, passionate woman standing before him with determination in her eyes and a defiant tilt to her chin.

"Are you sure?" he asked, praying she was. "I don't want regrets later."

That delicate hand of hers rested against his bare chest—just that simple gesture had his blood soaring. He ached for those soft hands of hers to be all over him.

"I have no regrets where you're concerned," she told him, her voice husky with arousal.

This was the moment he'd been waiting for…a moment he didn't think he'd ever be ready for after Andrea died. But he'd gotten stronger each day, had finally come to realize that he was still alive, that he needed to move on.

Drake reached around her and gave the door a firm shove to send it closing with a click. Then he fisted his hands in her hair and set his mouth over hers, needing to feel her.

Stepping fully against her, Drake slid his hands down her back to cup her rear and tug her hips toward his. Her purse and keys fell to the floor as her arms wrapped around his neck.

"It's late. I probably should've called," she muttered against his lips. "I just didn't think…"

"Good." He tugged her long-sleeved T-shirt over her head and tossed it to the side. "When you think you start to pull back. You followed your instinct, your heart. And you're in the right place."

Drake stepped back, ready to take his fill of the woman who had caused him many sleepless nights and cold showers. A shiver swept through his body.

"Are you sure?" she asked, holding on to his shoulders and studying his face. "I mean, I assume I'm the first since…"

"You're the first since Andrea passed," he confirmed. "I haven't wanted anyone else."

Marly closed her eyes. "I hope you're not disappointed. I'm not that experienced, and I just want you to—"

He cut her off with another kiss, then eased back. "Doubts have no room here. Deal?"

Nodding, she looked up at him and smiled. "Deal. But you'll tell me if you don't like something, right?"

"There's nothing you could do that I wouldn't like."

Marly's fingertips trailed over his chest, down his abs, and he nearly fell to his knees right there. He was so in for it. Any control he'd thought he had was gone and Marly held all the power. This beautiful, vibrant, vulnerable woman had more power than she could ever imagine. She might not realize how far she'd come since she'd first jumped beneath his touch, but she'd scaled mountains. Here she was, standing before him with all the confidence of a woman taking charge of her life.

Her courage was beyond sexy.

"I've only been with one man," she told him, eyeing the knot in his towel. "I'm just scared, I guess."

Tipping her chin up with his thumb and finger, Drake bent his head to look her in the eyes. "Don't do this because you feel like you have to."

"I want to be with you," she told him. "I want to move on. I want to prove to myself that I can do this and not be afraid, that there's a man who will treat me like I should be treated. But most of all I'm done denying what I want. I need you, Drake. I just need you to go slow. Is that okay?"

"You humble me." Drake framed her face. "I'm nervous I won't make this perfect for you."

Marly slid her hands inside his towel until it loosened and slid to the floor. "Just let me be in charge for now and I should be okay. If you start getting too dominating, that may scare me. I'm sorry."

Drake glanced down to where her hands had rested on his bare hips. "If you want to take charge, baby, I'm certainly not going to stop you."

Laughing, Marly went to unfasten her jeans. "I should've known you'd be fine with being manhandled."

"Handle me all you want." Drake spread his arms wide. "Where do you want me?"

Marly shoved her jeans down her legs, toed off her flats and kicked them aside, leaving her standing before him in a pale pink bra and panty set.

She glanced down at her body and shrugged. "Cotton, sorry. I wasn't planning on this when I got ready for the festival. But that's me, so…"

"They're coming off, so I don't care what they look like," he told her truthfully, though he would say anything to put her at ease.

"I'm not sure what kind of woman you're used to, but I hope the added weight and stretch marks are your thing," she joked, but her voice was laced with insecurity.

"Everything about you is my type of woman." He slid his hands over her hips and up to her waist. "No matter what you look like, no matter what battle scars you sport from a pregnancy or from defending yourself, you're the exact woman I want."

Marly trembled between his hands, but he slowly ventured on up and reached around her back to unhook her bra. With her eyes locked on his, she held out her arms as he slid the garment down and discarded it somewhere in the vicinity of the couch.

"I need you against me," he murmured as he splayed his hands across her back and pulled her body flush against his. "You feel so good, Marly."

Damn it, his hands were shaking. He didn't want

to mess this up, didn't want her to worry about doing something wrong or not living up to his standards.

What the hell had her ex filled her head with? The man had obviously been mentally abusive, as well. But there was no room for him in the relationship Drake and Marly were building, so Drake shoved all thoughts of the ex aside and focused on the nearly naked woman in his arms.

Hooking his thumbs into the waistband of her panties, he shoved them down as far as he could and let her take it the rest of the way as he nibbled on her throat.

Marly arched her back, her breasts brushing against the hair on his chest and sending jolts of need through his body so intense he was afraid he would snap. But he had to rein his desires back in and take all leads from her.

"Where's your bedroom?" she whispered.

"Too far away."

Molding her breasts in his hands, wanting to feel all of her at once, Drake walked backward until the couch hit the back of his legs.

Marly smiled up at him. "You ready?"

"Baby, I was ready weeks ago, the second you started lecturing me about the healing of burns."

Flattening her hands on his chest, Marly gave him a shove, sending him back onto the oversize couch. Looking up at her, with her swollen lips, her disheveled hair and totally naked body, Drake wanted to take a mental picture because he never, ever wanted to forget this moment.

Drake grabbed hold of her rounded hips and tugged

her to stand perfectly between his legs. Her fingertips dug into his shoulders as he dotted kisses along her abdomen.

After a moment, he rested his head on her stomach and closed his eyes. He was falling apart. Inside, where Marly had penetrated so deep, he was crumbling, because he wanted to be it for her. Not just her protector or even her lover, he wanted to be it. As in, happily-ever-after.

What an awkward time to come to that realization.

Drake breathed in and exhaled. No way could he confess this to Marly. He wanted her to stick around, not run away.

"You okay?" she asked, sliding her fingertips along his shoulders.

"Yeah," he said, his head still resting against her stomach. "I'm just trying to take it slow. I don't want to scare you, and I'm holding on by a thread here."

Her soft chuckle vibrated him. "I'm not scared of you," she murmured. "But we need a condom before this goes any further."

Condom. Yes. Why hadn't he thought of that? Oh, yeah, because he'd been finishing his shower when she'd knocked and he'd lost all rational common sense after that.

He came to his feet. "Don't move."

In a mad dash to his bathroom, he grabbed a condom, slid it on and returned to the living room, where Marly literally hadn't moved.

Instead of sitting back down, he took her into his

arms Rhett Butler–style, earning him a squeal and a slight laugh.

"What are you doing?" she asked, looping her arms around his neck.

"I changed my mind. I want you in my bed."

His bed, where no other woman had ever been. He'd replaced the bed he and Andrea shared, just another way he had moved on.

Marly's openmouthed kisses along his neck had him nearly growling as he gently placed her on his bed and came down to lie beside her. He was very careful not to put any weight on her.

He stroked her hip, the dip in her waist and traveled on up to one breast. Her bright eyes held his as she trembled beneath him. Knowing she trusted him with her body, her heart, was beyond humbling. This woman wouldn't be here if her heart wasn't invested… and that silent fact made him even more excited about where this was going.

When Marly reached down to stroke him, Drake's eyes nearly rolled back in his head. He eased away, falling onto his back, and laced his hands behind his head. She wanted control, fine by him. Who was he to stop her?

Damn, that felt good.

When she slid one leg over his and eased up to straddle him, Drake opened his eyes, not wanting to miss a second.

Marly smiled down at him and settled her hands on his chest. "You should know, I'm falling for you."

Drake swallowed. "Yeah? You should know I fell for you a while ago."

When she sank onto him and began to move, Drake knew she was the woman he'd been waiting for. He knew she was the woman he was meant to move on with. Now he just had to make sure she kept on this path, the path that led the two of them into a future together and away from her fears and insecurities.

Drake reached up, pulling her head down so he could capture her lips. Their bodies moved perfectly, her soft little moans filled the silence.

All too soon her body tightened, her fingertips bit into his shoulders and Drake let himself go, too. Finally. He'd finally found where he belonged.

Marly rested her head in the crook of Drake's arm. She'd tried to move more than once, but he'd silently kept his arm around her and tugged her back in place.

Tears pricked her eyes. The man was absolutely perfect. Well, no man was perfect, but he was perfect for her. She never knew a man could be so selfless, so genuine, with no hidden agenda. She'd been living in a shallow, loveless world for so long…and that was on the good days.

"Don't bring anything of your past into my bedroom," he whispered into the dark. "It's just us. There's nothing to fear. There's no one to hurt you."

Marly slid her hand up over his taut stomach and up onto his chest. "Sorry. Just thinking."

"I'd rather you be sleeping. It's after midnight and we had a really long day."

Sleep? At a time like this when she'd discovered she could fall in love, for real this time, and she had to figure out a way to keep Willow for good, as well as keep Drake off Kevin's radar? Sure, no problem falling to sleep with all of that swirling around in her mind.

"What was it like growing up with brothers and a loving family?"

Drake slid his hand up her bare arm and settled it on her shoulder. "You really want to just talk?"

"Yeah."

She'd never made love with someone and then just settled in afterward to appreciate the special bond. This was a moment she wanted to capture, because she'd never realized just what she'd been missing.

"My brothers and I may have caused a ruckus in town a time or two when we were teens," he started. His low voice caused his chest to vibrate. "My poor mother, she took it one day at a time. My father, on the other hand, wasn't so lenient. I know we embarrassed him on more than one occasion. He was the town doctor, so he was well respected. Then the St. John boys came through."

Marly fisted her hand on his chest and rested her chin there. "And here you all are with powerful jobs in the town. What transformed you?"

"As hellacious as we were, we respected our father." Drake slid her hair over her shoulder and smoothed it down her back. "Plus we all joined the service after we graduated. That pretty much knocked the chip off our shoulders."

He'd been a soldier, fighting for others. Just another

layer to his selfless ways. The man was remarkable in the fact he was always putting others first, proving beyond a doubt he was indeed a hero to anyone who came in contact with him.

Which made her wonder...

"Tell me about Andrea."

He stiffened beneath her, his heavy-lidded eyes closed for a brief second. "Are you sure you want that here?"

"I'm sure," she told him. "She's a part of you. I want to know about her."

With a sigh, Drake continued to stroke her hair. "We met when I came back home from the Marines. She was actually new to the area and was a professor at the college. She loved Nashville, but wanted a small town to settle in. We were set up on a blind date and we dated about two years before we became engaged."

Drake's eyes drifted across the room. "We were only engaged about a month before the accident. We were headed to a fund-raiser for the department. I was driving, she was in the passenger seat putting on her makeup and—"

"You don't have to go into that," Marly told him, placing a hand on his cheek to offer support. "I don't want you reliving it."

His eyes sought hers. "I relive it every day. But I'm to the point I can talk about it without all the survivor's guilt I once had."

"How did you get past that?"

"Counseling," he admitted. "I fought it at first, was convinced talking to a stranger wouldn't change the fact that Andrea was gone. I still have some guilt—I always will—but I realized that I couldn't have saved her. The accident was the fault of the semi driver who ran the light, not mine. She was pinned, and thankfully had passed out."

His chin quivered, sending a knife of remorse straight through Marly's heart. "Drake, please. I don't need to know any more."

Through the moonlight slanting across his bed, she saw the shimmer of tears in his eyes. "You're part of my life, Marly. I want you to know."

Flattening her hand over his heart, she waited for him to continue. This was important to him, perhaps even to his ongoing healing process. And he was right. She was part of his life now, no matter how frightening and thrilling that may be. If he wanted to share the most hurtful part of his past, then she would be brave enough to listen.

"The flames appeared before I could even try to get her out. The semi had tipped and was leaking gasoline."

Drake closed his eyes, a single tear slipping down his cheek. "The hardest part was getting out of that car, knowing she was trapped inside and there wasn't a damn thing I could do about it. That image… It haunts me. But I know had I stayed, I wouldn't be here."

Marly swiped Drake's damp cheek and turned his face until he met her gaze. "You're the most honorable man I've ever met."

Taking hold of her hand and kissing her fingertips, Drake smiled down at her. "I'll never let anyone hurt you. You know that, right?"

"When you say the words, I want to believe."

"Then believe it. I'm not afraid of what Kevin could do to me or my job. He tries anything in this town and he will have to answer for it."

Marly said nothing, letting the implications and this entire situation settle in. She truly believed Drake would do anything in his power to keep her and Willow protected. But she worried this was moving faster than she'd ever anticipated.

"I don't want you to think I want to be with you out of my need to protect," he said, interrupting her thoughts. "I'm not replacing Andrea with you and I am not attracted to you because I think you need saving."

Drake shifted on the bed, scooting up until his back was propped against his pillow. Marly sat up, too, facing him with the sheet pulled up over her chest.

"I'm perfectly aware that you can save yourself," he went on, taking her hands and settling them in his lap. "You've done a remarkable job for so long, but you don't have to be alone anymore. I want to be with you. I want to provide support both emotionally and physically."

Marly squeezed his hands. "I admit I'm tired. Tired of worrying, tired of wondering if he's going to find me today or if his lawyer and a corrupt cop are going to show up at my door and take Willow."

"What's the status of the courts and custody?" he asked.

Holding the sheet between her arms and her sides, Marly shook her head. "Right now I have full custody. He honestly doesn't care about Willow. She's too rambunctious, too tomboyish and too much work according to him. But he'll take her out of spite just because I love her and she's my world. Anything that hurts me would bring him joy."

Something glinted from Drake's eyes that hadn't been there a moment before. Something darker.

"He'll find me," she went on. "He needs me and Willow to stand by him for this upcoming election. He only waited because I threatened to go to the press about the abuse and he thought I'd come back on my own. Now that he sees I'm stronger and I'm not coming back, he's forcing his hand. He wants to play up the angle of how he's turned his life upside down to accommodate his family and how he's made every effort to reunite us."

The thought sickened her. She'd die before she ever returned to his clutches again.

"I refuse to go back, and when he finally comes after me, he'll be even angrier."

Drake tugged on her until she lay sprawled across his chest. Comforted by his strong arms wrapped around her, Marly slid her leg up over his firm thigh.

"I don't want to think about that tonight," she told him. "My worries will be there tomorrow, and reality is pretty harsh in the light of day. Can't we just have us right now?"

When she tipped her head to look up at him, Drake cupped her cheek, stroking her bottom lip.

"That's the second-best idea you've had."

Smiling, Marly eased up to straddle his hips. "And what was the first?"

"Showing up on my doorstep on a mission."

He gripped her arms and pulled her down for a toe-curling kiss. Marly shoved thoughts of anything else aside as she fell deeper in love with her hero.

Chapter Sixteen

"I'm pretty sure I have stale cereal or possibly a moldy loaf of bread," Drake mumbled as the sunlight flooded his bedroom. "So what would you like for breakfast?"

Marly rolled over and sat up, her back to Drake. "As tempting as that sounds, I need to go pick up Willow. Supposedly your mother is making her French toast."

The bed jerked behind her, and Marly glanced over her shoulder to see Drake jump up. "My mother is making French toast? Throw your clothes on and let's get going. You've never had a breakfast like that in your life, I guarantee it."

"I'm not barging in there and asking your mother to make my breakfast," Marly told him, still holding the sheet up around her chest. "I can grab something at home, but I don't want your mom to feel as though she has to keep Marly all day."

Shrugging as he pulled on his boxer briefs, Drake said, "Trust me, my mother doesn't care, and I'm sure by this point my dad is wrapped around Willow's little finger."

Marly tugged the sheet with her as she came to her feet. Her clothes were still strewn about the living room, which had seemed sexy and romantic last night, but in the light of day and after the fact, Marly was feeling more insecure than anything.

"Drop the sheet."

Marly turned to stare at the half-naked, beautifully sculpted man. "What?"

His eyes roamed over her body. "Drop it. I've seen everything you have and there's no way you're going to be insecure around me. Any imperfection in your mind is beauty in mine."

Marly clutched the sheet tighter between her breasts. Could she just drop it? For so long she'd been told how out of shape her body was, how the stretch marks could be removed if she'd get a tummy tuck. Added to that, Marly hadn't been naked in front of a man other than her husband before last night.

Drake crossed the room, slid his hands over hers and gently tugged until the sheet slid away and puddled at her feet.

"I don't care what happened before," he insisted, his dark eyes focused on hers. "I don't care what you've been told or how you've been treated. From now on, you'll be treasured, appreciated and loved. I don't want any doubts. I don't want any insecurities. Got it?"

Swallowing past the lump in her throat, Marly nodded. Drake's hands roamed up her stomach, over her breasts and up to her neck, where he used his thumbs to tip up her chin.

"We may be late for breakfast," he murmured against her lips. "I'm in the mood for something else right now."

Marly smiled. "You're going to make me look bad if I show up late to get my kid."

Wrapping his arms around her and tossing her back onto the bed, Drake crawled over her with a wicked grin and a quirk to his brow. "You're going to look really bad when we show up together. No way am I missing my mom's French toast."

Marly laughed as Drake started showing her his idea of breakfast.

Okay, so they were kind of late and more than likely breakfast was all gone, but the morning spent in bed had been so worth it.

Drake escorted Marly up the stone sidewalk toward his parents' house. They were running even later since Marly had insisted on grabbing different clothes from her house because she refused to do the walk of shame up to his mother's door…as if his mother wouldn't take one look at the two of them together and draw her own conclusions. The woman had raised three boys—she was pretty smart.

Drake eased around Marly and opened the front door. The instantly familiar smell of home greeted him.

Laughter and chatter came from the kitchen, and Drake grabbed Marly's hand, leading her that way.

"Wait," she said, tugging on his hand. "I am fine with your mom knowing about us, but let me talk with Willow. I don't want her to think I've just replaced her father or that this isn't something special."

Drake turned, framed her face with his hands and kissed her forehead before enveloping her in a hug. "I will do whatever you think is best for Willow. You just tell me what to do or what not to do."

Marly hugged him in return and stepped back. "I'll talk to her when we get home, so keep those lips and hands to yourself while we're here. Got it?"

Drake took a step away and saluted. "Got it."

"Mama!" Willow ran through the living room and launched herself at Marly. "Mrs. St. John makes the best French toast ever. I told her she could show you and you could make them again for me."

Drake couldn't help but laugh. When he turned to go find his mom, he ran into Cameron.

"Hey, didn't expect you here." Drake slapped his brother on the arm. "Cameron, this is Marly."

"Marly," Cameron greeted. "I've heard quite a bit about you."

"Glad I could finally meet the final St. John brother," she said, flashing a wide smile.

"Is Megan here, too?" Drake asked. "Haven't seen her much lately."

"She's been busy," Cameron replied. "I haven't got-ten much time in with her, either. Our friendship for the past few weeks has resorted to texts all hours of the day and night."

"Megan is Cam's best friend," Drake explained to Marly. "She's a therapist and has a very full schedule."

"Maybe I'll be able to meet her soon," Marly said, her weight shifting closer to Drake.

He slid a hand behind her back, silently stating just how serious they were. "You heard about Mom's French toast, too?"

Cameron shook his head. "Actually, I just got in from an all-nighter. I ran by here to see Mom and was heading to your place next before I run home and grab a few hours of sleep."

Drake glanced over his shoulder, saw Marly's questioning eyes on his. "I'll be back in in a minute."

"Everything okay?" she asked.

Drake nodded. "Yeah, just tell Mom I'll be right in."

With her hand on Willow's shoulder, Marly glanced between Drake and Cameron. "Okay."

Drake waited until she was in the other room and motioned for Cameron to follow. They stepped onto the porch and Cameron shut the door behind him.

Crossing his arms over his chest, Drake eyed his brother, who had circles beneath his eyes, wrinkled clothes, day-old scruff and disheveled hair. "You look like hell."

Raking a hand through his shaggy mop, Cameron sighed. "Trust me, I look good compared to how I feel."

Drake shifted his weight. "Man, you're killing yourself. I hope this case you're working on is ending soon. I've never seen you like this."

"It'll be over when it's over," Cameron muttered. "Anyway, I have information you need to know regarding your least favorite politician."

"I hope it's enough to keep him away from her."

"Maybe. I found a female who worked in his office several years ago. Supposedly she tried to file assault charges on Kevin, but then they disappeared and she suddenly left the office."

Drake gritted his teeth and glanced across the street as a kid went by on his bike and turned up a driveway. Another car pulled up to the curb a few doors down. Such a simple, mundane life he'd taken for granted, and Marly had endured hell. No more. He wanted this life for her; he wanted her to know simple and mundane.

Focusing back on Cameron, Drake asked, "So where is this woman now?"

"We're trying to find her," Cameron confirmed. "I should hear something in the next day or two. My friend is relentless, so he won't stop until he finds her."

"Good. I don't want Marly to know I'm having Kevin investigated." Drake glanced at the door, hoping his mother and Marly were bonding…or whatever women did. "He's been sending threats, and if he shows up, you better get there before I do."

"Oh, Drake, come on. Don't make me arrest you."

Drake fisted his hands on his hips. "If Marly and Willow are safe, I don't care what you do to me."

"Don't say that. Just let me handle this, all right?"

Drake merely stared, not saying anything else. Cameron knew full well that if Kevin stepped foot onto Marly's property, there would be no holding back for

Drake. He would protect what was his, and Marly and Willow belonged in his life now.

The swift revelation overcame him, and he knew right then that he would fight for her no matter what. He'd been given this second chance, and he wasn't going to throw it away because he was worried about his sometimes unsettling feelings.

There would always be that piece of him that missed Andrea. There would always be that piece of him that would wonder what would've happened if he'd been able to save her or if there'd been no accident at all. But he had to move on. Not just in small steps, but in this life-changing decision. At some point he would have to take a leap over that hurdle he'd placed before himself. So why not jump in and reach for the goal that was standing right before him?

"Dude, you all right?"

Drake glanced at Cameron, who was staring. "Yeah, sorry. Just zoned out for a minute."

"Anything to do with the fact you and the pretty nurse came to breakfast together?" Cameron asked with a knowing smile.

"Something like that."

Cameron smacked Drake on the shoulder. "Good for you. I knew you'd be able to fully move on once the right woman came into the picture. For what it's worth, and even though I just met her, I really like her. I'm a good judge of character, and Willow is a little pistol. She's adorable."

Drake couldn't help but smile. "She's pretty amazing, like her mom. I better get back in there. Keep me posted no matter how minor the information is."

Cameron nodded. "Will do. I'm headed home for a few hours of sleep before I hit the shift later. Text me if you need anything. Can't guarantee I'll get right back at you, but I will when I can."

"Just take care of yourself."

Cameron gave a mock salute. "Okay, Mom."

Drake gave him the one-armed man hug and headed into the house, where he found Willow on a stool at the sink washing dishes. Her nightgown sleeves were pushed up to her elbows, her bed head had been pulled up into a ponytail and she was just scrubbing away at the forks.

"This is how you wrap up a fun sleepover?" Drake asked his mother, who was putting fresh French toast onto plates.

"She wanted to do it," his mom defended.

Marly poured a cup of coffee and sat it in front of Drake. "Really, she loves doing dishes. She loves being a big girl and helping."

"I wanted to make the breakfast," Willow muttered with her back still to the room.

"It won't be long," Marly promised. "I'll have you making me breakfast all the time in a few years."

"So how was the sleepover?" Drake asked, pouring an insane amount of syrup onto his stack.

"Loud," his father said, stepping into the kitchen. "Those two laughed and talked until after midnight. I gave up and went to bed."

Drake saw Marly cringe, and he reached across the

table to pat her hand. "You're just jealous you can't stay up like you did when you were young," Drake told his father. "Put to shame by your wife and a little girl."

"Yeah, well, I found out that little girl is the best Go Fish player in the world." Mac St. John went over to the sink and patted Willow's head. "She beat me four times before I finally called mercy and asked her to leave me with some dignity."

Willow glanced over her shoulder. "He's really bad. I offered to give him lessons."

Marly relaxed a bit in her seat and started to cut into her breakfast. "Well, thank you so much for having her and for this amazing breakfast."

"Anytime," his mother said with a soft smile as she placed a couple of plates on the counter behind her husband for Willow to wash. "We loved having a young one in the house. Movies, cards, popcorn… We'll have to do it again."

Willow clapped, sending suds flying. "I can't wait!"

As much as Drake loved his mother's cooking, he couldn't help but sit back in his seat and take in the atmosphere of his parents bonding so easily with Marly and Willow. This was what he'd always wanted. When he'd grown up in this house, he'd known one day he would bring his family back here to spend time with his parents. Family meant everything to him.

Which meant now that Marly and Willow were part of his, he would stop at nothing to protect them and keep them safe. And soon he'd have to reveal to Marly that he wanted more. He wanted a future.

Chapter Seventeen

Marly had been home only a few minutes when her doorbell rang. Willow had just gone into her room to play, but knowing her daughter, she was probably worn out from the big night and would fall asleep amidst a pile of toys.

Marly headed toward the door, fully expecting to see Drake on the other side. But when she pulled it open, her heart literally jumped into her throat.

"Kevin," she whispered.

In a pale blue dress shirt and black pants, Kevin Haskins always looked like the smarmy politician he was. It nauseated her just to look at his flawless hair, perfectly manicured hands and that cocky way about him, now that she knew what lay behind the facade.

"I know I'm a day early, but I wanted to surprise

you," he told her with that sickening grin on his face as he pushed past her and looked around her living room. "I assumed you understood when I gave you another week that you would be getting ready to come home, but I can see you're not moving in that direction at all."

Marly glanced out the door onto the narrow street. Of all the times she wanted Drake to make a surprise appearance, this wasn't one of them. She couldn't let Kevin's and Drake's paths cross. She had to keep Drake protected, even though he was convinced he could handle Kevin.

"I see small-town life has changed you into a slob." His eyes raked over her hoodie sweatshirt and jeans. "Really, Marly. This is taking your independence a bit too far. Why on earth would you want to look like a suburban housewife with no care for herself?"

Marly crossed her arms and tilted her chin. "You need to leave."

Kevin jerked back as if she'd slapped him. Oh, the irony. She'd never talked back to him before. Never stood up and made a bold statement like that before. Damn...that had felt good.

"I'm not leaving," he all but laughed. "I'm here to get you and the girl and we're going back home."

Fury bubbled within Marly. "*The girl* is your daughter, and her name is Willow."

Rolling his eyes, Kevin sighed. "I don't have time for your games, Marly. For crying out loud, I had to drive all the way out here to retrieve you."

Retrieve her? Like she was a lost shoe?

"I'm not leaving, Kevin. We're divorced. No matter what you say to me, I'm not going with you."

Marly silently applauded herself for standing up to him. Years of marriage, being under his thumb and always being afraid to make him mad had weakened her. But since moving here, meeting Drake and seeing what love was, seeing how a man and woman should be together, Marly had a new outlook on Kevin, and she was ready for him.

"Hi, Daddy."

Marly turned and nearly cried. Willow stood at the end of the hall, almost as if she was afraid to come any farther. This was her own father, a man Willow hadn't seen in months. Just this morning Willow had been laughing and joking with a family that obviously loved her, and here the little girl stood before her own father and she was afraid to make a move.

All of those facts lined up to confirm that Marly had made the right decision in leaving and she'd made the right decision in moving on with Drake.

"Willow," Kevin said with a nod as if he were just greeting an acquaintance. "Your mother and I need to talk. You need to go play or something."

Willow looked at Marly and Marly offered a smile. "Go play, sweetheart. We'll build a fort in just a bit, so why don't you get all the blankets and pillows we need. Okay?"

"Okay, Mama."

Marly waited until her daughter was out of earshot before she rounded back on Kevin. "Don't be a jerk to your own daughter. I realize she's not what you wanted, but she's my world and you will respect her or leave her the hell alone."

Kevin stepped forward. Even though Marly wanted to step back, wanted to go straight into protective mode, she stood her ground. This was her house, her sanctuary, and he was not going to ruin what she was trying to build here. He was not going to come in and start taking charge. No more.

"My, my," he taunted as he continued to close the gap. "You've grown quite the backbone since you left. That's cute, Marly. Really. But we both know you'll come back to me."

"There's nothing you could do to make me come back."

That gleam in his eye made her nervous. Great, she'd just gone and basically challenged him. When he reached up to stroke her cheek, she gritted her teeth and held her gaze firm on his. She couldn't show any weakness or he'd completely turn this around and take all control.

"I'm sure I can get you to come back," he taunted as he continued to stroke. "I've known where you've been for a while now, actually. I know all about your little boyfriend. I know all about the young boy who was injured in the fire. I was at the festival yesterday. Across the street, actually, but I saw you."

Terror slid through her. He knew about Drake. Oh, no. Had he followed her to his house last night?

"You will come back," he continued, gripping her jaw with his crushing fingers. "Because I will donate enough money to this town to reinstate the men your boyfriend needs back at his department, and I will send a very generous check to the family of that boy who was injured. That's a lot of people whose lives could be changed for the better, all with one decision from you."

Marly hated him. She'd hated this man for a while, but right at this very moment she positively loathed him. She batted his hand away and took a step back.

"Get out of my house."

"I can see you're surprised by my generous offer. I'll give you two days to think about it before I come back."

As soon as he left, Marly's shaky legs gave out and she sank onto the floor. What would she do?

All of Drake's men would be back on the job, medical expenses would be not as much of a burden for Shawn and Amy and all Marly had to do was return to living in hell, living a nightmare.

"Mama," Willow called from the back bedroom. "I'm ready."

"Be right there, honey."

That sweet little voice, that precious, innocent little girl depended on Marly to keep her safe. There was no way she could return to the life she'd finally escaped from.

How could she fully explain this to Drake?

The two powerful men would inevitably meet. Marly only prayed Drake controlled himself, because the last thing Marly wanted was for him to be arrested by his own brother.

Drake pulled up to the curb at Marly's house with strawberry cupcakes. Apparently, when Willow had stayed over at his mother's house, the little girl had mentioned that her favorite dessert was strawberry cupcakes. He was such a sucker for a cute little girl with lopsided pigtails and cowgirl boots. He was a sucker for her mother, too.

Why hadn't he heard any news from Cameron? Not that Drake wished a woman to be another victim, but perhaps if the woman was willing to step forward, they could build some sort of case against Kevin so he would stay away from Marly. A man like that needed to pay, needed to be held accountable for his cowardly actions.

But right now, he was going to focus on building his future with this amazing woman who'd swept into his life and instantly had him reevaluating his priorities. She'd put light into the darkest corners of his heart he never thought could be touched again.

And sweet Willow thrown into the mix was just the cherry on top.

Drake held the cupcake box in one hand, rang the doorbell with the other and was a bit surprised when Marly's soft tone came from the other side of the door.

"Who is it?" she asked.

"It's me."

The dead bolt slid back, a chain jingled against the door and finally the door opened. He knew she'd been frightened, but this was a first for all the locks and her extra security.

She turned when he entered. After closing the door behind him, Drake glanced around. "Where's Willow?"

"She's in my room watching a movie." She still kept

her back to his. "We were having movie night and I was about to make some popcorn."

When she went into the kitchen, Drake followed again. He sat the cupcake box on the kitchen table, wondering why this felt so…off. Something was wrong.

"I brought strawberry cupcakes," he told her, watching as she reached up into a cabinet to grab a box of popcorn. "My mom said Willow mentioned they were her favorite, so I thought she may like some."

"That's sweet. I'll go get her."

Her clipped words, her lifeless tone had Drake crossing the small space and grabbing her elbow until she turned to face him.

When he caught sight of her pale face, her swollen eyes, fear gripped him. "What happened?"

That quivering chin of hers nearly did him in. "It's nothing. I just have a lot on my mind."

"You've been crying. Talk to me."

Her face searched his and for a moment he thought she'd open up, but she shook her head. "I… It's nothing."

So they were back to that. Disappointment slid through him, making him wonder how they could've taken such giant steps forward and suddenly be taking more steps back. She'd erected that wall again.

Hadn't she just left his bed that morning? Was she having delayed regrets? Something other than the usual issues was troubling her enough to bring her to tears. And not just a few tears, but enough to have her eyes puffy and red.

"If you shut me out again, I can't help you," he whispered.

Marly's face crumbled, and he quickly wrapped her in his arms. Before he could do much more than run his hands up her back, Willow, with her lopsided pigtails, came skipping into the kitchen.

"Hi, Chief. Why is Mama crying?"

Marly started to straighten, but Drake held her tight. "These are happy tears," he explained with a smile, hoping she'd buy the lie. "She was so excited about the strawberry cupcakes I brought, she just started crying."

Willow's eyes scanned the kitchen until they landed on the box on the table.

"Can I have one?" she cried.

Marly sniffed into his chest as Drake continued to stroke her back. "Sure," he told her. "Go ahead and take it on back, but try not to make a mess, okay?"

Quickly, she tore into the box and chose the perfect cupcake and raced from the room.

"I hope you don't mind you're probably going to have strawberry-cake crumbs in your bed."

"I don't mind." Marly wrapped her arms around him. "I'm sorry. I don't mean to fall apart on you. I was back there in the dark and Willow didn't notice I was upset. I thought I could keep this to myself, but..."

Easing back just a bit, Drake tipped his head to the side to peer down at her. "But what?"

Wet eyes came up to meet his. "I need you. I thought I could do this, I thought I could save you, but I can't do it alone."

"Save me?" he asked.

Marly bit her trembling lip and glanced away for a

moment. But that was enough for Drake to see the round bruises along her jaw.

Stroking the spot lightly with his finger, Drake asked, "What's this?"

A deep breath sent a shudder through her body that shook him. "Kevin was here earlier."

Rage like Drake had never known rolled right through him. "He was here? He put his hands on you?"

"Please, stay calm," she pleaded, a fresh round of tears filling her eyes. "I can't do this if you're going to get all Neanderthal on me."

Barely able to rein his temper back in, Drake nodded. "Fine. Did you at least call the cops?"

Marly shook her head. "He wasn't here but just a few minutes."

"Enough time for him to put his hands on you." Drake glanced at the bruises again and nausea settled deep in his gut. "Damn it, Marly."

"I wanted to handle this all myself," she told him, easing back and wrapping her arms around her waist. "I didn't want to run to you to save me or you to ride to my rescue, but he gave me an ultimatum."

Drake didn't give a damn what this ultimatum was, he was going to track down Kevin and see just how well he liked having someone else's hands on him. Drake couldn't wait to meet the man and finally put this nightmare for Marly to an end.

"What did he say?"

Drake almost didn't want to know what this man was threatening Marly with now.

"Basically he wants me to come back and when I

cooperate he will donate enough money to your department to reinstate the three men you had to lay off, plus he'll make a very generous donation to Shawn and Amy for medical bills."

Drake cursed beneath his breath and gripped her shoulders. "You do understand you're not going back? No matter what he promises, you will not go back to him."

Marly nodded. "I know. I battled back and forth. I could save several jobs and help Shawn and Amy, but at what cost? I can't put myself in danger again and I refuse to bring my daughter back into that hell."

Drake let out a breath he hadn't realized he'd been holding. At least she was thinking straight and not trying to play hero by sacrificing herself.

"I'll notify Cameron." He held up a hand when she opened her mouth. "I'm just letting him know Kevin is in the area and that he threatened you. I'll need those pictures you have, and I want to take pictures of your jaw."

"It's just a bruise," she told him. "There's no need for a photo."

Meaning she'd lived through worse, and that thought infuriated him. "It needs to be documented that he was here for a short time and already put his hands on you."

Drake clenched his fists at his sides, trying to control his fury. She didn't need to see that; she needed him strong and thinking rationally. "I need those pictures," he told her. "I need to show Cameron."

Marly nodded and left the room. By the time she'd come back, Drake had almost calmed a tad, but then he took one look at the images and gritted his teeth so hard his jaw popped.

"I want you to let Cameron handle this," she told him, placing a hand on his arm. "I don't want Kevin to ruin your career, which is already teetering on a thin line with the mayor. And I want this to be handled the right way. I need Kevin to stay away from Willow."

Drake nodded. "I won't mess this up, Marly. He will be taken care of properly."

"He was so cold to Willow," she whispered. "No hug, barely a hello. I know he hates me and wants to control me, but she's his own flesh and blood. How can he be so heartless?"

"He won't be a problem again, Marly. I swear." Drake wrapped her in his arms again. "I'm staying here to-night."

This wasn't up for debate, and he wasn't asking. No way in hell could he go back home and leave these two on their own.

Marly gripped his shirt and held on tight. "I was hop-ing you'd say that."

Finally, he'd fully penetrated that wall of defense. Now if he could just handle Kevin, get his job back and convince Marly they belonged together long-term, he'd be all set.

One hurdle at a time. The first thing he would take care of was the ex. No way would that man lay another finger on Marly again.

Chapter Eighteen

Drake convinced Marly to call off work Monday morning, and he personally drove Willow to school, briefly discussed the issues with the principal and alerted him to potential problems with Kevin. Though Drake didn't think the lowlife would be brazen enough to show up at the school, Drake wasn't taking any chances at all with the family he'd come to think of as his own.

Back at Marly's house, she was a cleaning machine. Apparently she was relieving stress by sweeping, dusting, scrubbing showers and mumbling to herself as she went from room to room.

Drake ducked out onto the front porch to call Cameron. He figured his brother would be in the midst of either heading to the station or crawling into bed. Quickly dialing the police chief's cell, Drake took his gaze from one end of the quiet street to the other. Nothing out of the ordinary stood out, but then again he highly doubted a coward like Kevin would show his face with Drake here. Kevin was the type of man who opted to only prey on innocent women and children. No way would he actually want to go up against someone who would put up a fight.

"Yeah," Cameron answered.

"Kevin showed up at Marly's yesterday."

Cameron cursed under his breath. "Did he do anything to her?"

Images of those fresh bruises marring her skin had that pit in his stomach tightening all over again. Not to mention the pictures she'd brought out to him. He would never get those images out of his mind. Her nightmares were now his, and he planned on taking them away from her for good.

"He left some bruises," Drake informed his brother. "She's fine, but he did try to blackmail her into leaving. He's using me as the material."

"Real powerful man to use a woman as his shield to get through life. Let me call my investigator and I'll be over there in about an hour. I want to see those pictures and see Marly's new injuries."

"We aren't going anywhere."

"Have you thought about taking her to your house?" Cameron suggested.

"Apparently the bastard has been in town awhile. He knows where I live, I'm sure. Besides, Willow is used to this being her new home and I don't want her scared or confused."

"Understood," Cameron replied. "Be there as soon as I can."

Drake hung up, knowing his brother was running on empty, but also knowing there was no way Marly and Willow could get through this time alone. The sooner they got the threat of Kevin out of the way, the sooner they could move on with their lives.

Drake also had the council meeting tonight, but until this issue was resolved with Marly, he refused to leave. He would make calls, write letters or send someone in his place, but he wasn't leaving his family.

Yes, they were his. He'd grown to love them, cherish them and would always put their needs first. Starting with tonight and missing the meeting. If he lost his job over protecting his family, then so be it. He'd find other work. As much as he loved firefighting, he loved Marly more.

He wasn't going to let another person he loved slip through his fingers when he could save her, build a future with her and love her forever.

Ready to fight for another chance at love and happiness, Drake vowed to let nothing stand in his way.

Marly was utterly humiliated. She sat on the edge of the ottoman in her living room while Drake and Cameron pored over her pictures and asked her questions.

This was why she wanted to handle Kevin on her own. For one thing, she hated for anyone to see that side of her. The broken, vulnerable, helpless side.

For another thing, the look in Drake's and Cameron's eyes, the anger and fury that poured off them, scared her. She wasn't worried for herself, but feared what they would get into if they approached Kevin.

Kevin certainly wasn't a man to use violence against other men; he was too much of a coward for that. But he could use his power, his name and his old money to influence nearly anybody.

"Get that look off your face," Drake scolded.

"I was just going to tell you the same thing." Marly crossed her arms and leaned forward over the tops of her knees. "I don't care what you do by legal means, but do not start a fight, and please don't risk your careers. Either one of you."

Cameron shook his head. "You aren't the first battered wife I've seen or talked to. But I will say you are the first one that has really hit close to home with me. I won't risk my career, but I won't let Kevin continue to threaten you, either. He'll be dealt with properly."

Drake practically fumed, but Marly trusted them both to heed her request.

"Can I take these?" Cameron tapped the images on the table. "I promise they won't get away from me and no one who isn't pertinent to the case will see them."

Marly chewed her lip, knowing that this was too big for her to handle on her own. "Okay."

Cameron came to his feet. The poor guy looked so worn out and absolutely exhausted. Drake had mentioned that his brother was working some intense undercover case. Marly couldn't imagine laying your life on the line every day for your job.

"I need to speak with you outside," Cameron told Drake. "We'll just be a minute."

Once the guys left, Marly went to get the money bag from the festival. With all the unexpected chaos, she hadn't been able to get the cash deposited in order to write Shawn and Amy a check.

She'd counted all of the bills and was separating out the change when Drake came back in. Whatever he and Cameron had discussed had at least relaxed him a bit.

"Well, you've stopped clenching your jaw," she murmured. "That's a good sign."

He turned a kitchen chair around backward and straddled it. "I totally forgot about counting this. I'm sorry."

Shrugging as she stacked quarters into neat piles, she said, "No big deal. I'm almost done."

By the time he pitched in and they finished, they had more than either of them had thought in the first place.

"This will be a nice surprise for them," Drake told her. "We can bring the check over tomorrow if you'd like. I think Shawn said he would be at the store tomorrow and Amy would be there on Wednesday."

Marly nodded. "Sounds good. I want to get it to them as soon as possible. Why don't you go ahead and take out the money you put in for supplies?"

Drake pushed up from his seat. "Absolutely not."

Glancing up, Marly sighed. "You put in a good bit of materials for flyers, signs around town and quite a few other things."

"I won't take a dime from this, and I'll actually be adding to it."

Noble to a fault. The man was also stubborn, but how could she not admire and love every part about him?

"Need I remind you that you're suspended with no pay right now?"

Drake offered her a crooked smile as he reached for her hands and pulled her to her feet. "No need to remind me, but I also have a nest egg in savings. I'll be fine. They need the money way more than I do anyway."

Marly reached up, stroked his stubbled jawline and returned his contagious smile. "So what did you and your brother talk about?"

Drake's hands came around to her backside; he pulled her flush with his body and nipped at her lips. "Now, why would I want to talk about my brother when I've got a beautiful woman in my arms?"

Marly didn't miss the way he'd totally dodged the question, but the way he held her, the way he cherished her had her realizing this was so much more important than whatever they'd discussed.

"I'll let you skip the question," she murmured against his lips. "But only because this feels too good."

Running his arms up the back of her sweatshirt, Drake's fingertips expertly flicked her bra open. "Things are about to feel a whole lot better."

"But what if—"

Drake cut her off with a kiss. "Don't say his name. He's not coming as long as my truck is here, I'd guarantee it. Right now it's only me and you. Willow won't get picked up from school for a couple hours now and I want to be with you, just you, with nothing else getting in our way."

Marly wrapped her arms around his neck and arched into him. "Then why are we wasting our time talking?"

Drake took her words to heart when he stripped her down in record time and hoisted her up onto the kitchen table. To know she had such control over him that his own control snapped sent a quick bolt of arousal through her. Never before had she been so reckless as to have sex on her kitchen table in broad daylight, but Drake didn't seem to mind as he removed all of his clothes and piled them with hers across the kitchen floor.

As frenzied as Drake was at the start, when his hands slid up her body and to her face, he was so gentle, so... soft. Those fingertips glided over where she knew those bruises were.

"Nothing else but us," she reminded him.

He captured her lips and pulled her forward until she wrapped her legs around his waist. "Always us," he murmured as he joined them together. "Always."

Chapter Nineteen

Drake had dropped Marly and Willow off at Eli and Nora's house. He wasn't comfortable leaving them alone and he had business to attend to.

Granted, he was on his way to find Kevin, but Drake still didn't think leaving Marly alone was a good idea. For one thing, she didn't know he was going to see Kevin and Drake didn't want her worrying about him. For another, Drake had no clue what minions the creep may have brought with him, so he wanted to cover all his bases.

Oh, the bastard had no clue Drake was coming, or that his police chief brother was meeting him there. The element of surprise was on his side, and he fully intended to keep the upper hand at all times from here on out.

Cameron had informed him earlier that morning that Kevin was staying just outside of town in a nicer hotel that was closer to the city. Of course he wouldn't want to degrade himself and stay at the local hotel that was family owned.

Drake had also learned quite a bit about the woman who had originally filed assault charges against Kevin… the charges that had suddenly disappeared were surprisingly found once Cameron's investigator started digging deeper.

Drake entered the hotel, met Cameron in the lobby and followed him toward the elevators.

"My investigator said Kevin is staying in Room 801. It's a suite, of course."

Drake clenched his fists, still not sure exactly what he'd say to the man who'd made Marly's life a living hell for years. Not to mention the fact that he'd utterly ignored Willow…which was probably a good thing, except for the fact he was using the innocent child as a pawn to lure her mother back.

"You may want to simmer down a bit," Cameron muttered as they stepped into the elevator. "We're just presenting him with his options."

Drake snorted. "Options? He has one. Leave Marly the hell alone and get out of town."

"Why don't you let me talk?"

Drake shot his brother a narrowed look as he exited the elevator. No way in hell would he let Cameron fight his battles. Cameron was here as a witness, to make sure Kevin understood all the damning evidence they had uncovered. And to make sure Drake didn't kill him.

Cameron tapped on the door and Kevin opened it just enough to peer beyond the chain. "Yes?"

Cameron flashed his badge. "Stonerock Police. I need to speak with you, Mr. Haskins."

Drake loved the authority in his little brother's voice. Loved how Cameron could put the fear of God in so many people.

"What can I do for you?" Kevin asked, still not opening the door any wider than the chain would allow.

"I just have a few questions for you, sir. Would you mind if I came in for just a minute?"

Drake stayed off to the side; there was no way he wanted Kevin to see him. Although, if the man were smart, he'd already know that Cameron was Drake's brother, but Drake wasn't anticipating that Kevin had done a great deal of homework on Marly's new life. He had tunnel vision, and that tunnel led straight to the election. "I suppose," Kevin said.

The door closed while the locks were cleared away, and Cameron shot Drake a look. "Stay calm or I'll pull you out of here," he whispered.

Drake nodded. As much as he wanted to go charging into that room and tear Kevin apart, Drake wouldn't do anything to put Marly in any danger or jeopardize her case in the custody proceedings.

When the door swung open, Cameron stepped in first, and just as Kevin was about to close it, Drake slammed his hand on the door and pushed his way through.

Kevin's eyes widened. Oh, yeah. The jerk knew exactly who Drake was. Good.

"Mr. Haskins, come have a seat," Cameron said, breaking through the tension.

Kevin's wide eyes jerked to Cameron. "You said you were with the police."

"I said *I* was," Cameron corrected. "My brother is the fire chief…but you probably already knew that."

Drake closed the door behind him, keeping his eyes on Kevin the entire time. "You'll want to sit down. We may be a while."

Kevin went into the living area and took a seat on the navy sofa. Dressed in black dress pants and a dark gray shirt with the cuffs turned up, Kevin looked like a typical polished businessman. Unfortunately, Drake had seen photos that proved this man was anything but typical or polished.

Arms crossed over his chest, Drake leaned against the TV stand directly across from Kevin. Cameron took a seat in a wing-back chair and held up a folder.

"This contains some pretty damning information, Mr. Haskins," Cameron started. "First of all, I know you visited Marly yesterday."

Kevin laughed as he eased back on his cushy sofa. "You're wasting my time because I visited my wife?"

"Ex-wife," Drake quickly corrected, barely managing not to leap across the room and punch the smug smirk off Kevin's face. "She divorced you when you beat her and didn't take her for treatment and the wound on her head didn't heal properly."

Kevin narrowed his gaze at Drake. "Is that what she told you? She's always fabricating stories."

Cameron reached into the folder and held up a photo

of Marly with a bloody head. "Did she fabricate the pictures, too? That's a lot of work to go through for one story."

Kevin eased forward, his confident demeanor starting to crack. "What do you want?" he asked.

"It's not what I want," Drake chimed in before Cameron could go all cop on him. "It's what is going to happen. You will leave Marly alone. She isn't coming back to you. You also will drop this custody battle, because you don't give a damn about your own daughter."

With a laugh, Kevin shook his head and sighed. "Who is going to stop me from taking everything I want? You two? Aren't you suspended from your job? What power do you hold anyway? And your brother is a small-town cop who can't do a thing to me for visiting my own wife. Your threats are wasted here."

He started to rise and Drake took a step forward. "Sit down."

Obviously the tone did the trick because Kevin eased back into place. Drake rested his hands on his hips, continuing to stare the other man down.

"I have a statement from Janet Days that states you assaulted her when she worked in your office back when you were a lowly commissioner." Cameron pulled out a sheet of paper. "Here it states exactly what you did to her and her injuries, and she even reported that she feared her accusations would disappear and nothing would come of it."

Kevin tensed, and suddenly that cocky smirk was gone, replaced by fear. Drake still wanted to pummel the man.

"It's her word against mine," Kevin defended. "And apparently the police didn't take her seriously."

"Interesting," Cameron went on, holding up a hand to Drake, who had just pushed away from the TV cabinet. "My investigator also found another woman who was working in your office only two years ago who said the same thing. I have to say, Mr. Haskins, these ladies who don't know each other at all, both had quite similar stories."

Kevin came to his feet. "Get out. You can't arrest me and I won't say anything without my attorney anyway."

Drake shot across the room, his fist connecting with Kevin's jaw until the man fell back onto the sofa.

"Damn it, I told you to stay calm," Cameron shouted.

Shaking his hand, Drake shrugged. "I was calm for nearly ten minutes."

"I'll sue you," Kevin whined. "I'll press charges."

"I'll arrest him if you want me to—"

Drake smacked Cameron's shoulder. "The hell you will."

"But," Cameron continued, looking between Drake and Kevin, "I think you'll want to hear everything I have to say before you make any decisions about pressing charges."

Cameron stepped between where Kevin was rolled into the corner of the couch holding on to his jaw and Drake.

"These ladies I've found have agreed to come forward and testify against you if you choose not to leave Marly alone," Cameron stated. "Once they heard about your wife and why she truly left you, they were all too eager to discuss their forgotten cases."

Kevin narrowed his eyes. "She's my wife."

"She's your ex-wife and your former punching bag." Drake gritted his teeth. "And you'll drop the custody case, too, because we both know you don't want Willow. You've never been a hands-on dad, and she wouldn't be comfortable with you anyway. For once, think of the child."

Drake wasn't leaving this room until he was satisfied Kevin was out of Marly's life for good. He refused to let this jerk hold any power over Marly for one more second of her life.

"So what do you say?" Cameron asked, stepping forward and looming over Kevin. "You ready to get yourself back to Nashville and leave this town for good?"

Kevin glanced from Cameron to Drake. "You can have her. She's not worth the fight."

Drake stepped around his brother, came right to the edge of the sofa and leaned down within a few inches of Kevin's swollen face. "She's worth everything. You were just too cowardly and arrogant to realize that."

"Get out," Kevin spat. "I won't come into your ridiculous town again, but threaten me again and I'll have both of your jobs."

Drake laughed, pushing away from the couch. "You don't have a leg to stand on, Haskins. The charges we can bring against you would ruin any pitiful reputation you think you've built. So take your threats and get the hell out of Stonerock."

Pushing aside Cameron and maybe stepping on Kevin's feet, Drake headed to the door. "I'm done with this garbage."

He stormed out of the room before he really did something stupid like punch the man again. Because as good as it had felt to hit him once, Drake truly wanted to go full-on assault on the loser.

But, having respect for Marly and not wanting to stoop to Kevin's level, Drake was ready to close this chapter and move on. Drake knew the Nashville PD already had a warrant waiting for Kevin when he arrived back home, because Cameron had called a contact he knew for sure wasn't corrupt to handle the case. Kevin wouldn't be hurting any more women, and he certainly wouldn't be running for reelection.

Drake glanced at his watch and realized there was no way he'd make the council meeting.

Drake waited at the elevators for Cameron. If Drake had to go to the city offices tomorrow and explain why he was absent, he would. But right now, all he cared about was getting to Marly and building up a solid foundation for their future.

He was so quiet on their way home from Eli's house. Whatever had happened while he'd been gone had really upset him.

Marly let herself into her house and asked Willow to go on back and start getting ready for bed. Marly needed a few minutes alone with Drake.

After he closed the door behind him, he sighed and leaned against it.

"You weren't reinstated, were you?" she asked, almost afraid of his answer.

His brows drew in as he pushed off the door. "What?"

"The council meeting that was tonight. They sided with the mayor, didn't they?"

Drake closed the space between them and rested his hands on her shoulders. "I didn't go to the council meeting. I honestly have no clue what they've decided."

"What? Where were you?"

Those intense eyes held hers as he squeezed her shoulders. This couldn't be good. Fear pitted in the depths of her stomach.

"Drake?"

"I went to see Kevin."

Her entire world tilted. Marly swayed just as Drake's arms came around her. There was no way he'd gone behind her back and gone to see her ex-husband.

"Sit down." Drake ushered her to the couch where he sat down beside her. "Before you get upset, please hear me out."

"Upset?" she repeated, clasping her shaky hands in her lap. "I'm not upset, Drake. I'm hurt you didn't tell me that was where you were going. You let me assume you were going to fight for your job."

He gripped her shoulders and turned her to face him fully. "I went to fight for you, which was a hell of a lot more important than any career."

If she didn't love the man before now, the fact he'd laid literally everything on the line for her had her heart tumbling over in her chest.

"Do I want to know what happened?" she asked, almost afraid of his answer.

Drake tipped his head and offered her a grin. "The CliffsNotes version is Kevin is out of your life. You don't have to worry about anything else."

Questions, scenarios bounced around in her head. "What about the custody? I can't let Willow—"

Drake's finger covered her lips. "Taken care of. When I say I'm going to take care of what belongs to me, I mean it. I had Cameron do some digging, and he uncovered more women who stepped forward, willing to give their statements. The Nashville police are waiting for him and he won't be a problem for you anymore."

Tears instantly pricked her eyes. "I can't believe you'd do this for me."

His hands framed her face. "I did it for us," he said, sliding his lips over hers. "I did it because I love you."

A shudder rippled through her, vibrating against his body. "Oh, Drake," she cried, clutching him tight. "I love you. I love you more than I thought I could ever love a man."

He nipped at her lips again. "That's good, considering you'll never be without me."

Chapter Twenty

Standing outside this house that had once served as her prison, Marly smoothed her dress down and knocked on the door. She was ready once and for all to face her past and move on. With Kevin's power, he'd been given house arrest until the arraignment. She needed closure, needed him to see that she was strong, needed to prove that any power he'd ever had over her had disappeared. Most of all, she needed to put their marriage behind her so she could move on with her new life…her happy life.

The wide mahogany door swung open, and Kevin stood before her. One side of his face was swollen and bruised. Shock registered first, followed quickly by a sense that Drake had doled out his own brand of justice.

"What do you want?" Kevin growled. "I already told

your boyfriend and his brother I was out of your life for good."

Oh, the images that flooded her mind of Kevin facing down two St. John boys were almost comical.

"I heard that you opted to be smart for once." Marly smiled, knowing full well for once in her life, where this man was concerned, she held the upper hand. "I'm here to make sure you are fully dropping the custody dispute with Willow. I want to hear you say it."

His eyes narrowed. Well, one eye was nearly swollen shut, but the other one narrowed into a slit. "You can raise your kid any way you want," he told her. "You've ruined me and my career."

Crossing her arms over her simple wrap dress, Marly shrugged. "I think we both know who's to blame for your career spiraling out of control."

"Get the hell out of here, Marly."

Oh, yes, the fact that he was afraid shouldn't make her feel so happy. But for once in his life, he was scared of something, and that something was her and the power she now had over him.

And because she was feeling so powerful and wickedly happy, Marly took a step forward and stared him straight in the eyes. "If you come near me or my daughter again, I can't promise what Drake did to your face won't seem like a day at the beach."

As she turned on her heel and left this house for the final time, Marly realized she'd never felt so liberated, so free and happy in all her life.

Now she could truly start building the life, the family she'd always wanted.

* * *

Drake had never been so nervous in all of his life. He stood outside of Marly's house and rang the doorbell. The sun was just starting to set, and he hoped he wasn't interrupting dinner.

Willow answered the door and her sweet smile hit him square in the heart. "I have a loose tooth," she declared as she opened the door. "I've been wiggling it all day."

The innocence of a child. Drake stepped into the house and instantly smelled something baking.

"This is your first loose tooth," he told her, squatting down to look into her mouth. "What a big deal."

Willow nodded and snapped her mouth closed. "I can't wait for the Tooth Fairy. I might get a whole dollar like some of the kids in my class."

Laughing, Drake came to his feet just as Marly stepped into the living room, wiping her hands on a towel.

"Drake." Her smile spread across her face. That smile reached her eyes, and for the first time showed no sign of fear or worry. "I was going to call you in a bit to come over."

He hadn't been able to stay away. Not after he'd come to a life-altering decision.

"Hope I'm not interrupting."

"Not at all." She turned to Willow. "Go finish wiping off the table, please."

Willow ran past her mother and into the kitchen. "We're baking cookies," Marly said.

"You're always baking something."

"Well, these are chocolate chip, and I happen to know a certain firefighter who loves homemade cookies." She tossed the towel onto her shoulder. "What brings you by?"

"I wanted to know if you and Willow would like to go look at a litter of puppies with me."

Her face lit up. "Oh, you're getting a dog? That's great. Willow would love to go look at puppies."

Drake swallowed, knowing this moment was going to change his life…one way or another.

"I have a friend who found a litter on the side of the road and he's looking for homes for them." Drake ran a hand across the back of his neck, never dreaming he'd be this anxious or nervous about being there. "I also wanted to run by my house to show you the addition, now that it's nearly done. I need a woman's opinion on the paint color. I'd actually like Willow's opinion."

"Willow's opinion?" Marly laughed. "Be prepared for a shade of blue or green."

"That would be fine with me." He stepped forward, taking her hand in his. "I was also hoping that once I get the puppy I want and take him home, that maybe you and Willow would like to come home with me, too… you know, permanently."

Marly's eyes widened, then watered. "Drake," she whispered.

He dropped to his knee and pulled the box from his pocket. "I got this the other day, but I wanted to wait until you were ready. I don't expect you to answer me right now, but will you wear my ring? Will you consider moving in with me and the new addition can be Willow's room? Will you marry me one day?"

Marly dropped to her knees as well, and clasped her hands around Drake's and the box. Instead of answering his questions, she said, "I went to see Kevin earlier."

Fear threatened to creep up. "What?"

"I'm not scared anymore," she told him. "I'm not afraid to move on, to let you help me face my fears. Willow and I were planning on bringing you the cookies and telling you that I'm—we're—ready to move on. With you."

Relief swept through him. He took the ring from the box and slid it onto her finger. The thick band with a simple inset of diamonds fit her perfectly.

His hands shook as he held on to hers. "I saw this set and it looked just like something you'd wear. Simple, elegant."

Those watery eyes came up to meet his. "It's perfect. You're perfect."

"Why are you guys on the floor?" Willow asked, coming over and trying to wedge herself between them.

Drake laughed. "Because we're weird," he explained. "What do you say to helping me pick out a dog?"

"Seriously?" she asked.

Drake nodded. "I also need you to pick out your favorite paint color because I have a new room, and it can be yours, if you want."

"We're going to live with Drake," Marly explained. "Mama and Drake are getting married. What do you think of that?"

Willow let out an ear-piercing squeal that penetrated

his eardrums. "A loose tooth, a puppy, a new room and a cool new dad all in one day? This is the best day ever."

Drake kissed Marly over Willow's head. "I couldn't agree more."

* * * * *

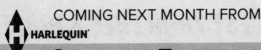
#2389 MENDOZA'S SECRET FORTUNE
The Fortunes of Texas: Cowboy Country • by Marie Ferrarella
Rachel Robinson never counted herself among the beauties of Horseback Hollow, Texas...until handsome brothers Matteo and Cisco Mendoza began competing for her attention! But it's Matteo who catches her eye and proves to be the most ardent suitor. He might just convince Rachel to leave her past behind her and start life anew—with him!

#2390 A CONARD COUNTY BABY
Conard County: The Next Generation • by Rachel Lee
Pregnant Hope Conroy is fleeing a dark past when she lands in Conard County, Wyoming, where Jim "Cash" Cashford, a single dad with a feisty teenager on his hands, resides. When Cash stumbles across Hope, he's desperate for help, so he hires the Texan beauty to help rein in his daughter. As the bond between Cash and Hope flourishes, there might just be another Conard County family in the making...

#2391 A SECOND CHANCE AT CRIMSON RANCH • by Michelle Major
Olivia Wilder isn't eager for love after her husband ran off with his secretary, leaving her lost and lonely. So when she scores a dance with handsome Logan Travers at his brother's wedding, her thoughts aren't on romance or falling for the rancher. A former Colorado wild boy, Logan is drawn to Olivia, but fears he's not good enough for her. Can two individuals who have been burned by love in the past find their own happily-ever-after on the range?

#2392 THE BACHELOR'S BABY DILEMMA
Family Renewal • by Sheri WhiteFeather
The last thing Tanner Quinn wants is a baby. Ever since his infant sister died, the handsome horseman has avoided little ones like the plague—but now he's the guardian of his newborn niece! What's a man to do? Tanner calls in his ex-girlfriend Candy McCall to help. The nurturing nanny is wonderful with the baby—and with Tanner, too. Although this avowed bachelor has sworn off marriage, Candy might just be sweet enough to convince him otherwise.

#2393 FROM CITY GIRL TO RANCHER'S WIFE • by Ami Weaver
When chef Josie Callahan loses everything to her devious ex-fiancé, she leaves town, hightailing it to Montana. There, Josie takes refuge in a temporary job...on the ranch of a sexy former country star. Luke Ryder doesn't need a beautiful woman tantalizing him—especially one who won't last a New York minute on a ranch. He's also a private man who doesn't want a stranger poking around...even if she gets him to open his heart to love!

#2394 HER PERFECT PROPOSAL • by Lynne Marshall
Journalist Lilly Matsuda is eager to get her hands dirty as a reporter in Heartlandia, Oregon. The locals aren't crazy about her, though—Lilly even gets pulled over by hunky cop Gunnar Norling! But the two bond. As Gunnar quickly becomes more than just a source to Lilly, conflicts of interest soon arise. Can the policeman and his lady love find their own happy ending in Heartlandia?

YOU CAN FIND MORE INFORMATION ON UPCOMING HARLEQUIN® TITLES, FREE EXCERPTS AND MORE AT WWW.HARLEQUIN.COM.

HSECNM0215

***

Matteo knew he should be leaving—and had most likely
already overstayed—but he found himself wanting to linger
just a few more seconds in her company.

"I just wanted to tell you one more time that I had a very
nice time tonight," he told Rachel.

She surprised him—and herself when she came right down
to it—by saying, "Show me."

Matteo looked at her, confusion in his eyes. Had he heard
wrong? And what did she mean by that, anyway?

"What?"

"Show me," Rachel repeated.

"How?" he asked, not exactly sure he understood what she
was getting at.

Her mouth curved, underscoring the amusement that was already evident in her eyes.

"Oh, I think you can figure it out, Mendoza," she told him. Then, since he appeared somewhat hesitant to put an actual meaning to her words, she sighed loudly, took hold of his button-down shirt and abruptly pulled him to her.

Matteo looked more than a little surprised at this display of proactive behavior on her part. She really was a firecracker, he thought.

The next moment, there was no room for looks of surprise or any other kind of expressions for that matter. It was hard to make out a person's features if their face was flush against another's, the way Rachel's was against his.

If the first kiss between them during the picnic was sweet, this kiss was nothing if not flaming hot. So much so that Matteo was almost certain that he was going to go up in smoke any second now.

The thing of it was he didn't care. As long as it happened while he was kissing Rachel, nothing else mattered.

***

Don't miss MENDOZA'S SECRET FORTUNE
by USA TODAY bestselling
author Marie Ferrarella,
the third book in
THE FORTUNES OF TEXAS: COWBOY COUNTRY
continuity!

Available March 2015, wherever
Harlequin® Special Edition books and ebooks are sold.

HARLEQUIN®
A *Romance* FOR EVERY MOOD™

**Stay up-to-date on all your
romance-reading news with the
Harlequin Shopping Guide,
featuring bestselling authors, exciting new
miniseries, books to watch and more!**

The newest issue will be delivered right to you
with our compliments! There are 4 each year.

Signing up is easy.

EMAIL

ShoppingGuide@Harlequin.ca

WRITE TO US

HARLEQUIN BOOKS
Attention: Customer Service Department
P.O. Box 9057, Buffalo, NY 14269-9057

OR PHONE

1-800-873-8635 in the United States
1-888-343-9777 in Canada

Please allow 4-6 weeks for delivery of the first issue by mail.